Darkling Green

Also in the series

Eldritch Manor
Shadow Wrack

Darkling Green

The Eldritch Manor Series

Kim Thompson

DUNDURN
TORONTO

Printer: Webcom

Library and Archives Canada Cataloguing in Publication

Thompson, Kim, 1964-, author
        Darkling green / Kim Thompson.

(The Eldritch Manor series)
Issued in print and electronic formats.
ISBN 978-1-4597-3622-1 (paperback).--ISBN 978-1-4597-3623-8 (pdf).--
ISBN 978-1-4597-3624-5 (epub)

        I. Title.

PS8639.H62676D37 2016   jC813'.6   C2016-902729-5
                                                 C2016-902730-9

1   2   3   4   5   20   19   18   17   16

We acknowledge the support of the Canada Council for the Arts and the Ontario Arts Council for our publishing program. We also acknowledge the financial support of the Government of Ontario, through the Ontario Book Publishing Tax Credit and the Ontario Media Development Corporation, and the Government of Canada.

Care has been taken to trace the ownership of copyright material used in this book. The author and the publisher welcome any information enabling them to rectify any references or credits in subsequent editions.

— J. Kirk Howard, President

The publisher is not responsible for websites or their content unless they are owned by the publisher.

Printed and bound in Canada.

VISIT US AT

 dundurn.com |  @dundurnpress | dundurnpress | dundurnpress

Dundurn
3 Church Street, Suite 500
Toronto, Ontario, Canada
M5E 1M2

for Lizzie (my April Fool)

Cast of Characters

Willa Fuller — Twelve years old, or to be specific, almost, *almost* thirteen. An "ordinary" girl who discovered this extraordinary house quite by chance. Clever, brave, and responsible. Has recently discovered mental powers she never knew she had: she can communicate telepathically and sense other people's emotions.

Willa's Family
Belle (full name: Mirabelle) — Cranky old mermaid in a wheelchair. Self-centred and blunt. Willa recently learned that Belle is her long-lost grandmother. Long ago, Belle assumed human form to marry a handsome fisherman. She grew dissatisfied with life on land and returned to the ocean, abandoning her husband and young daughter, Maris.

Grandpa (George Godwin) — Willa's grandfather, a fisherman who singlehandedly raised Willa's mother after Belle left. Jovial and full of life. Also gentle, kind, and forgiving. Doesn't like to dredge up the past.

Maris Fuller (née Godwin) — Willa's mom. A bit of a control freak, stern and strict. Dearly loves her family, with the exception of Belle, against whom she holds a gigantic grudge, even after all these years. She's got her own secrets, and she keeps them well.

Marvin Fuller — Willa's dad. Shy and retiring. There's no drama in his past, and he'd rather avoid the drama in his wife's family altogether, thank you very much.

Inhabitants of Eldritch Manor

Baz — Short, stout old lady who loves to take catnaps. Her past is a mystery, but it has become apparent that she is more cat than human, despite her appearance. Has a special interest in charms and magic.

Horace — A bookish and mild-mannered old gentleman. Thousands of years old. Prefers birthday cakes *without* the candles, for fire safety reasons. He also happens to be an androsphinx. This means he is able to assume the form of a lion, though he prefers his boring human shape. Recently, his memory has begun to fail him, with nearly disastrous results.

Tengu — An elderly, pint-sized martial arts master with a very big heart. Human in form, his age is advanced but indeterminate. Always cheerful and full of childlike enthusiasm. Has an unhealthy obsession with lethal weaponry.

Darkling Green

Mab — Queen of the fairies. Keeper of dreams, mistress of enchantments, Mab is a dainty spitfire and imperious ruler of all the fairies of the backyard. She is combative and stubborn, and her past is about to catch up with her.

Sarah — A young, lively fairy, Sarah is the plucky personal assistant to Mab. When she began this job she was devoted and dutiful, but over time has become less impressed with her royal taskmaster. Not the greatest knitter around.

Robert — Irascible old fellow with a quick temper. He is a centaur, human from the waist up, with the body and legs of a horse. Cannot change shape, which makes it pretty difficult for him to blend into a crowd.

Miss Trang — Stern middle-aged lady who is supposed to be caretaker-manager of Eldritch Manor, though Willa is left in charge whenever she wanders off. Miss Trang occasionally turns into a massive fire-breathing dragon.

Roshni — A phoenix, descendent of an ancient line. A bird of prey, she is the size of a large hawk and has recently been living in the wild. Quietly devoted to Willa.

The dwarves — Nine capable workmen hired by Miss Trang to rebuild Eldritch Manor. Though sometimes inscrutable, the dwarves have hearts of gold and are artists and engineers of incredible skill. Mjodvitnir is the leader, Fjalarr his right-hand dwarf. The others are Radsvidr, Vindálfr, Svíurr, Aurvangr, Dólgthrasir, Hlévangr, and Eikinskjaldi.

Chapter One

"It's a good time to be Zen," observed Tengu one crisp November day as he flung razor-sharp ninja stars into the stable wall. THWACK! THWACK! THWACK!

"Absolutely." Willa stood under a tree, holding a shoebox as the little fairy Sarah flitted back and forth from a hole in the trunk, bringing out Mab's belongings and packing them in the box. The fairy queen herself was reclining on a branch nearby, looking bored.

"Meditation and solitude," continued Tengu, prying the stars out of the wood. "My inner peace has been seriously disrupted by recent events."

Willa nodded. It was now two weeks since the terrific battle of Hallowe'en night, and things had finally settled back to normal around town. Rumours of a fierce lion roaming Hanlan's Park had died down, and even Mr. Hacker had decided it must have been some kind of trick-or-treat prank. And if anyone had managed to catch a glimpse through the fog of an immense bird with massive claws and the back legs of a lion battling a fire-breathing dragon … well, they weren't talking. It was all over now, and Willa was ready for a blissfully uneventful winter.

Tengu continued pitching ninja stars into the wall. THWACK! THWACK! THWACK!

"How exactly does that help your 'inner peace'?" asked Willa with a smile.

The old man looked at her in surprise. "I derive much joy and satisfaction from handling weapons. Don't you?"

"Not really," answered Willa as Sarah dropped a load of clothing into the box.

Mab sat up suddenly. "Roll the scarves or they'll wrinkle!"

"Yes, Your Royal Weariness," Sarah sighed.

"What was that?" Mab snapped.

"Royal Fairyness. I said, 'Yes, Your Royal Fairyness.'" Sarah winked at Willa as she pulled filmy bits of spider-web scarf from the shoebox and rolled them up. Willa hastened to change the topic.

"Are you sure you want to move into the house, Mab? The other fairies are staying out here in the woods."

Mab sniffed. "Trees are summer homes. I am far too delicate to stay out here in the cold."

"But we don't have a dollhouse for you yet."

"Mimsy and Cowslip found a home for me," answered Mab, perking up. "It's a little rustic but highly portable. I can hang it anywhere I like. Here it is now."

Willa turned to see four fairies fly up carrying a dusty grey ball between them.

"A wasp nest? Is it … empty?"

Mab smiled. "The wasps were *persuaded* to find other accommodations. Don't you love the design? Very modern. Just like the Guggenheim."

The fairies brought it closer, and Willa gingerly put her eye to the round hole that served as a door. The inside had been emptied out, leaving a simple, papery orb with walls thin enough for the light to glow through. "Very nice," she admitted.

Just then Robert came trotting through the trees. "The dwarves are ready," he announced. "It is time for the unveiling of the first floor!"

Sarah flew out with a final armful of tiny shoes and dumped them into the box. "That's everything!"

Willa shut the lid as Sarah and Mab flitted off, accompanied by the fairies with the wasp nest. Willa followed slowly, enjoying the crackle of leaves under her feet and the autumn sunshine slanting through the trees. Everything was quiet and still.

Willa rounded the house and joined the others in the front yard. She was glad the tall construction fence hid them from the street, because they were certainly a bizarre-looking group. Robert the centaur clip-clopped around with pint-sized Tengu at his side, hopping up and down with excitement. Horace stood behind Belle in her wheelchair, her mermaid tail glistening in the sunshine. Baz, stout and grey-haired, was lying in the grass, watching everyone through half-closed eyes. Fairies buzzed around in the sunshine, their wings a fuzzy blur.

"Is everyone here?" Robert looked around. "Where's Miss Trang?"

Just then she appeared, approaching from the other side of the house. Miss Trang was moving very slowly these days, almost like she was underwater. Willa shook her head. It didn't look right at all.

"Is she okay?" she whispered to Belle.

"Yes, yes. She gets like this every winter. Dragons don't like the cold, you know," Belle answered.

"But most of the time she's human."

"Doesn't matter. Inside she's a cold-blooded reptile," Belle remarked, then added hastily, "I mean that in the best way possible, of course."

Everyone waited as she approached. And waited. Leaves floated down around them. Baz began to snore. At last Miss Trang reached the front walk. "What are you waiting for? Let's go in," she said with a yawn.

"Come on, Baz, time to wake up!" Tengu grasped Baz's hands and tried to haul her to her feet, but she went limp and slithered out of his hands to the ground.

"Baz! If you can't stand up, someone else will get your room, and you'll be sleeping outside this winter!" snapped Belle.

Baz opened her eyes and sullenly raised her wrists. Tengu grabbed them, stepped on her feet, and pulled her upright. Willa smiled and gazed around at the odd group of friends. *Her* friends. She felt a sudden, intense fondness for them all. The feeling grew in her chest until she could hardly breathe.

"Look!" Tengu pointed. A large bird circled down toward them, landing lightly on the gatepost. Its feathers glinted in the sunshine.

"Hello, Roshni," said Willa.

"Splendid! The phoenix has come back to us," said Horace. "I'm sure there's room for her here. In our home." Everyone fell to chattering excitedly about Eldritch Manor. Willa gazed up at the house.

From the smoking ruin of three months ago, progress had certainly been made. The walls of the first floor were complete, and above that white posts rose in a skeletal description of the second storey to come. The basic beams of the place were growing up out of the ground on their own; the dwarf construction crew was merely filling in the gaps between them. There was still a lot to be done, but with the cold weather coming, Willa was glad that at least the main floor was ready for residents to move in. Robert's room in the basement had been finished first, so Horace, Tengu, and Belle had crowded in there with him for the last two weeks. They curtained off a private corner for Belle, which was awkward, but Belle had stoutly refused to return to Willa's house, since she and Willa's mom were still not speaking. Baz was here, there, and everywhere, a portly old dame roaming the back alleys with her ragtag gang of neighbourhood cats. Miss Trang, well, nobody knew exactly where she'd been staying. She kept largely to herself, though now she was slowing down so much that it would be good to get her safely inside. The dwarves had promised rooms on the first floor for Horace, Tengu, Belle, Baz, and Miss Trang, though as Willa looked at the structure, she wasn't sure how all of them could fit in there.

"Right. Let's get started." Robert smoothed down what was left of his white hair before clopping awkwardly up the front steps and onto the porch. The heavy wooden door featured an ornate knocker, which Robert now struck loudly.

He stepped back as the door swung open. Nine dwarves solemnly marched out, lining the porch. Willa thought they'd spruced themselves up a bit. At the very least they had washed their hands and wiped their grimy faces. A couple even wore bowties atop their ancient leather work aprons.

Last to exit was their leader, Mjodvitnir, who bowed low and intoned, "I, Mjodvitnir, son of Vestri, descendent of a long line of dwarf craftsmen and artists, am proud to present Eldritch Manor, Phase Two."

He turned and led the way inside as everyone crowded up the steps to the door. Willa put Mab's shoe-box into Belle's lap, took the handles of the wheelchair, and pushed her around to the new ramp at the side of the porch. They entered the house just before Robert, who took up the rear.

It was dark inside after the bright sunshine, and Willa walked right into a chandelier, a mass of dangling glass prisms hanging at eye-level. Edging her way around it, Willa saw that the front hall was wide and spacious, but with a very low ceiling.

"Um, isn't the chandelier a little big?" she hazarded to Fjalarr, one of the dwarves. He smiled and shook his head.

"The house will grow into it. You'll see." He then strode to the middle of the hall.

"Ahem! Ladies, gentlemen, Little Folk. I welcome you to the opening of this, the next phase of Project

Eldritch Manor. To your left you'll find the parlour, featuring Tournesol Windows with cutting-edge sunbeam-bending technology! Sunlight streams in all day!" This elicited oohs and aahs from the company. Fjalarr continued. "The parlour opens into the dining room, and beyond that is the kitchen, which is still out of bounds. Bit of a work-in-progress mess, if you know what I mean…."

Then the dwarf gestured to the floor of the front hall. Willa noticed there was a large square cut into the floorboards.

"At your feet, convenient basement access." Fjalarr put his hand on an intricately carved dragon topping the bannister post at the foot of the stairs. He flicked open the dragon's mouth, and with a quiet rumble one end of the trapdoor began to lower. Everyone jumped back as it descended and came to rest, forming a ramp to the basement. Robert's eyes lit up.

"Wonderful! May I?"

Fjalarr nodded, and Robert stepped forward, experimentally clopping down the ramp and back up again. Then he flipped the dragon's mouth shut. The ramp rose and clicked back into place.

Robert grinned with delight. "Brilliant!"

Next Fjalarr turned and swept his arm grandly to the other side of the hall. "On your right you will find what you've really been waiting for. Your rooms will eventually be located on the second and third floors, but we have arranged temporary quarters for you down here. They're a little unusual, but I trust they will serve."

There was silence as those assembled viewed the five doors. They were right smack beside each other, with no space between them at all.

"How large are these rooms?" queried Belle. "They don't look big enough to swing a cat in."

Baz narrowed her eyes and hissed. "Just a figure of speech, dearie," Belle added quickly.

"Their size shifts as required," explained Fjalarr. "Go in, and you'll see what I mean."

Each wooden door had a small carving in the centre: a lion's head, a cat, a winged dragon, a mermaid, and finally an emblem with crossed daggers.

"That one's mine!" chortled Tengu. He hopped forward and swung the door open. The room was simply furnished, with a bed, dresser, and bookshelf, and as Fjalarr had said, it was a normal-sized room.

Belle's door was right next to Tengu's, and she protested immediately. "If his room is that big, mine must be a shoebox!"

She pushed her door open, but the room within was the same size as Tengu's. Horace, Baz, and Miss Trang opened their doors, and they too were faced with equally large rooms. Willa gazed from one doorway to the next. She couldn't make the spaces add up in her mind. They should overlap, shouldn't they?

"It's a clever new method of building temporary portable rooms. The only downside is that they can be a little, er … shifty," admitted Fjalarr.

The residents discovered what he meant when they woke the next morning to find the walls had crept right up to the sides of their beds. The walls retreated when they got out of bed. Tengu discovered that if he jogged in circles, he could make his room expand to the size of a gym. Baz's room, on the other hand, was usually broom closet–sized, since she never slept there. She preferred the sofa in the parlour, where she could be found snoozing at all hours.

Belle, Horace, Miss Trang, and Tengu settled happily into their new rooms, and Mab had her modernist hive hung in a corner of the parlour. At first it hung above the sofa, but Baz liked to sit on the sofa back and bat at it until Mab tumbled out, livid with anger but too dizzy to give Baz a proper zap. So the nest was moved to a spot across the room where Baz couldn't get at it, and at night it glowed in the dark like a patio lantern.

Willa brought over the large birdcage from her house, but Roshni seemed so happy roaming about the house "free range" that she decided not to cage her.

Roshni wasn't the only unexpected return. The first night that frost was forecast, Willa heard a faint tapping at the front door and opened it to find the hibiscus, a little limp but still green, sitting there on a black ball of earth and roots.

"Oh my goodness! I'm so sorry, I forgot all about you," said Willa. She carefully repotted the plant and placed it on the mantle next to a large ceramic bowl. This bowl contained a fairy-sized silver scarf, very small knitting needles, and the most valuable item in the entire house: a tiny ball of silver yarn about the size of a raspberry. This yarn was Eldritch Manor's time talisman, and Mab spent every day knitting it into a scarf to keep time moving forward. As the hours passed, the stitches at the bottom pulled out; Mab had to keep knitting new rows so it wouldn't disappear entirely. If that happened, Eldritch Manor and everyone within the bounds of the property would be ripped out of human time, deposited into a grey void. That alone was frightening enough, but if the evil creatures from the dark side ever managed to steal that ball of yarn, it would allow them to come and go at will in the human world, wreaking all kinds of havoc and destruction.

Willa peeked into the bowl and poked at the yarn with her finger. It didn't make sense that something so tiny could hold that much power. Then again, Willa had to admit that nothing about Eldritch Manor made much sense.

Chapter Two

Telepathy, phobias, and siren song

As November drew to an end, the temperature dropped, and Miss Trang continued to slow down. When Willa chatted with her, she had time to count the seconds between each word. One day she counted four seconds, a few days later eighteen seconds, and when it hit twenty-seven, Willa started avoiding her. She felt bad about it, but it was just too hard to remember what they were talking about for the length of an entire sentence. Miss Trang didn't seem to mind; she withdrew from the life of the house and rarely emerged from her room.

Tengu spent most of his time jogging around the park, or stalking and pouncing on invisible foes in the yard. The dwarves continued work on the second storey. They also removed the high construction fence to give back the view of the street but put up fencing at the sides of the house to keep the backyard private.

Robert hosted convivial evenings with the dwarves, and the others sometimes joined in. Ancient card games were played, and a goodly volume of red dwarvish port was consumed.

For his part, Horace never played cards. He preferred to sit by the fire and observe the others. His memory lapses used to cause him much anxiety, but after the recent uproar he had become much more philosophical about it all. Whenever he couldn't remember something, he'd simply sigh and smile. He told Willa it was foolish for anyone over two thousand years of age to get fired up over simply growing old.

"It behooves one of my advanced years to be more serene about the travails of existence," he would say dreamily and smile. "There's no point in flipping out over what I can't change." Willa noticed too that the others had become more protective of him. Whenever Horace grew confused, they — Belle and Baz mostly — drew near, taking his hand in theirs and reassuring him with their presence.

Whatever might befall his memory, Horace's sense of humour remained intact. One day, he and Willa were out for a walk, and they ran into Mr. and Mrs. Hacker, their tremendously irritating neighbours. Horace showed no signs of recognizing them, but after they passed by he leaned over to Willa, and whispered, "I know perfectly well who they are, I'd just rather *not* know, if you catch my meaning."

Since the eventful night on Hanlan's Hill, the Hackers had kept a wary distance. Willa knew Mr. Hacker had been quite shaken by those strange events, not the least of which was having his car crushed by a falling boulder. He even seemed a little frightened of Horace and Willa, often crossing the street to avoid them, which suited them just fine.

Willa had recently discovered she was able to send mental messages to people, an ability that filled her with pride but also made her a little anxious, because she didn't really understand how it could be possible. She felt she shouldn't let too many people know about it yet, but decided she could confide in Horace.

"Do you remember on Hanlan's Hill, how I talked to you with my mind?" she asked him one day.

"Yes."

"I've been wondering how I did it. How does it work?"

He looked surprised. "In the usual way, I suppose."

"This isn't exactly *usual!*"

"What do you mean? Don't all humans have this ability?"

"No!" Willa laughed.

"Well, that puts it in a different light," Horace said slowly. "It must be due to the renegade in your family tree."

"You mean Belle?"

"Most certainly. Would you like some assistance with your telepathic communications?"

"Yes, please."

And so Horace began to help her strengthen and control this power. They'd sit across from each other and send mental messages back and forth. In the beginning, Willa could only do it slowly and with great effort, but with practice it came easier, and they held many a long, effortless conversation without uttering a word.

"It's as easy as talking!" Willa marvelled one day. "I hardly know I'm doing it!"

Horace shook a warning finger at her. "Be mindful. Do it with intent and not just for a lark." He sat back wearily. "Don't overuse it. All powers come with a price."

"What kind of price?"

"It's not always obvious what you are losing. Not right away." He rubbed his forehead. "Many would disagree with me and insist that a special ability has no downside, but I feel in my heart that something is lost whenever you gain a powerful skill like this." He turned to look out the window, and Willa knew he was thinking about his own memory loss. She promised herself she'd practice her ability but not use it lightly. And she never mentioned it to anyone else.

A few doors down from Horace was Belle's room. The mermaid was very pleased to have her own space again; she was much more relaxed and less cranky. The porch ramp allowed her to wheel herself out the front door and down into the yard, which she couldn't do on her own before. The dwarves even paved a walkway for her that circled the house and branched off to the stable and woods. Not that she went into the woods much; Belle regarded the fairies there as nuisances, too foolish to bother with.

Willa knew Belle liked her privacy, but she gingerly began visiting every day after school, tiptoeing through the dusty disaster zone of the kitchen and making tea, then knocking on Belle's door. Belle's scowl would vanish when she saw it was Willa, a fact that Willa noted and cherished. They sat together over tea, and Willa found that if she didn't ask too many questions, Belle would start talking on her own. She didn't talk about Grandpa or Willa's mom, but for the first time she told stories about her early years under the sea, stories about castles on the ocean floor and bizarre creatures of the deep, about playing hide-and-seek in waving kelp beds and hitching the occasional ride on a manta ray. She often said she'd love to show Willa these things.

"I don't swim," Willa always replied, but Belle never seemed to hear it. She was fixated on the idea of taking Willa swimming, and Willa didn't have the heart to tell her it could never, ever happen. The embarrassing truth was that Willa was scared of the water. Make that terrified. It was some kind of phobia, and her mom had it too.

"We both have this condition, Willa," her mom always said. "I've had it all my life. If we tried to swim, we'd freeze up with a panic attack. It's a phobia, it's all in the mind, but the physical effects are real, and I don't want *either* of us to drown! So please stay out of the water!"

When they were at Grandpa's house on the beach, Mom didn't even like it when Willa kicked off her sandals to dip her toes in the ocean. Willa waded a little bit, but only up to her knees. If she went any deeper, she was gripped by a panicky, tight feeling in her chest. She couldn't breathe, and her limbs became leaden and useless. Her mom was absolutely right; there was no way she could will her arms and legs to move and swim once that feeling came upon her. It was all she could do to stumble backward out of the water and rejoin her parents on the towel in the sun. There she'd sit, staring at the sparkling water. The thought of all the creatures and fish and plants that were hidden out there beneath the shimmer creeped her out.

Belle's whole world revolved around water, and Willa was scared to death of it.

One day, Belle told her she used to pull pranks on human ships.

"What kind of pranks?" asked Willa.

"We'd get them going in the wrong direction, sailing in circles, or sometimes send them into the rocks."

Willa started. "You mean wreck them?"

Belle looked uncomfortable. "*We* didn't wreck them, exactly, we'd just get them going toward the rocks. If the sailors couldn't figure that out in time, well …" Belle shrugged.

"Wait, how did you 'get' them going the way you wanted? What do you mean?"

"Siren song," she said simply, pouring another cup of tea.

"You sing, and—?"

"Any men who hear it do whatever we want them to do. It's hilarious."

"You can do that?"

"Of course! Every mermaid worth her salt can."

"I don't believe you."

Belle laughed and plunked down her cup. "Okay then, miss smarty-pants. I'll prove it."

Willa followed Belle outdoors and around to the backyard, where they found Robert and the dwarves in the middle of a dispute over a game of horseshoes.

"It was a clear ringer. A perfect shot!" insisted Radsvidr.

"Doesn't count if your big fat toe is over the throwing line," countered Robert.

The dwarf stomped up to Robert, craning his neck to glare up at him.

"It wasn't!"

Robert leaned a long, long way down until they were eyeball to eyeball.

"It … was!"

"Wasn't!"

"Was!"

"Wasn't!"

"Was!"

"Wasn't!"

Horace was leaning against the house, smiling affably at Willa and Belle. "Such is the level of debate here," he observed.

Belle smiled, then cleared her throat and began to hum. In just a few seconds the argument died away, and they stared blankly at each other.

"I'm sorry. What were you saying, my good man?" asked Robert mildly.

"I've lost my train of thought," the dwarf answered, scratching his head. They looked at each other for a moment.

"Thirsty," mumbled Belle, just loud enough for Willa to hear.

Robert blinked and smiled. "Oh well, no matter. I'm parched. How about a beverage, old sport?"

"By all means. Lead on, friend."

Willa stared as the two strolled away.

"Told you," said Belle simply.

"It just works on men?"

"Yes, unfortunately. You know, *all* mermaids can do this…." Belle gave Willa a meaningful look, but Willa was thinking about something else.

"That's what you used on the policemen and the firefighters, isn't it?" she exclaimed. "That night at Hanlan's Hill!"

Belle smiled broadly. "No comment."

Willa nodded, impressed. "Wow. That must come in handy."

Belle sighed, glancing back at the house. "I'm not supposed to use it at all — Miss Trang's rules. It's for the best, I suppose. Siren song usually causes more trouble than it's worth."

"How?"

Belle had her hands on the chair's wheels and was turning back to the house. She paused for a moment before answering.

"People stop trusting you when they think you can control them."

Belle rolled slowly along the walk, and Willa watched her go. *People like Grandpa, I bet,* she thought.

Chapter Three

Silent, soft, and slow descends the snow

Of course Willa didn't spend all her time at Eldritch Manor. She went home for supper and to sleep, though whenever she had a spare moment before or after school, she wandered over to the old house see her friends. It was a strange notion that she would rather have tea with old folks than hang out with kids her own age. Her schoolmates found it strange, that's for sure, and they started to write her off. The strange silvery streak in her hair didn't help. It had appeared suddenly the day Eldritch Manor burned down, a mark that set her apart from normal people. Willa found it funny that her mom was more anxious about her "fitting in" at school than Willa herself was, and the streak in her hair drove her mom nutty.

"We can dye that out," she said two or three times a week, but Willa refused. She liked to be different from the other kids. She didn't even mind that she was no longer a part of their world. Well, not much anyway. It's true she occasionally missed talking to other twelve-year-olds, but she had nothing in common with them anymore.

Now Willa preferred to sit back and observe the other kids, and soon found she could detect things about them. Not their exact thoughts or anything like that, but if she kept her own mind very still, she could feel what they were feeling. It was like hearing very faint music from another room. This new skill fascinated her, but she had to stay apart from the chatter and interaction to do it. Soon she was fading into the background so effectively, it was almost like she was invisible.

It's easier this way, she thought.

As for her time at Eldritch Manor, the more she got to know the seniors there, the more she enjoyed their company. The sulky moods and childish tantrums were now few and far between, but even those ratty moments had become rather dear to Willa. She was unaccountably fond of them all; their bad behaviour just made her love them more.

Days at Eldritch had become much simpler. The old folks were calm — there were no outright wars, anyway — and with everyone back in the house, they were pretty content. And in a stroke of luck, the Hackers had left for the winter months, off to a sunny southern beach or something. Keeping a houseful of magical creatures secret from nosy neighbours is pretty much a full-time job, and Willa was relieved to be free of them for a while. With fewer worries, she slept better at night, and the extra sleep enabled her to think clearly, do better in school, and develop her new telepathic skills.

Even her home life was calm and happy. With Belle, Baz, and the bird Roshni all out of the house, it was just her, Mom, and Dad once more. Everyone relaxed, and it was nice to be around her parents again. Mom and Belle weren't exactly friends, a fact that used to drive Willa crazy, but now she knew that wasn't her problem, really. It was their battle, and they might never see eye-to-eye, which would be sad, but at least Willa had both of them in her life, and she was immensely grateful for that. And while they weren't talking, at least they weren't staring daggers at each other when they accidentally found themselves in the same room. That was a step forward, anyway.

The only thing that niggled at the back of her mind was that trouble always seemed to pop up, eventually. Trouble in the form of extremely evil beasts and monsters from the dark side that were always circling, just out of sight, ready to pounce. Willa resolved to stay vigilant and watch for any signs of them. She clung to a vague feeling that, after the last battle on Hallowe'en night, she and her friends could handle nearly anything if they stood together.

This was the state of things when the snow came. In mid-December it began to fall, more snow than the town had seen in many years. It drifted down, soft and silent, all night long, and the sun rose on sparkling snowbanks and snow piled high on every available surface: roofs, cars, fences, power lines, railings, posts, clotheslines, mailboxes. The scene was jaw-droppingly beautiful.

That afternoon, Willa shuffled through the snow, creating two parallel tracks all the way to Eldritch Manor and enjoying the puffs her breath made in the air. She entered the front hall, stamping the snow from her boots, and walked right into the chandelier. As usual. She bonked into that thing every time she came into the house.

"Aaargh!" She reached up to steady it and looked into the parlour. Horace was gazing out the window.

"Hi, Horace. Isn't the snow amazing?"

"It wasn't me," he blurted, starting a little.

"What wasn't you?"

"Nothing." Horace pursed his lips like he was holding in a secret.

"Horace … what have you been up to?" said Willa with a smile. "You look guilty of something."

Horace looked out the window again, wincing. "I was fiddling with some weather charms, but I really don't think… This is probably not my doing," he ended quickly.

Willa laughed. "If it *is* your doing, I'm impressed! I love it."

Horace looked very pleased. "You don't think it's too much? I just wanted a picturesque dusting of snow, not record-setting heaps of it."

"You don't know your own strength," Willa said, pulling an afghan off an armchair and draping it over his shoulders. Horace grinned brightly.

"Hmph!" tinkled a little voice behind them. "I HATE the snow!"

Willa turned to see Mab sitting in the bowl on the mantle, knitting away.

"Hello Mab, how's it going?" Willa walked over and lifted the scarf, which was about the length of her arm. "You've been busy!"

Mab paused to flex her fingers. "I have to knit to keep warm! Wretched winter!" She gave Horace a nasty look.

"It most likely has nothing to do with anything I was doing," he protested weakly.

Skritch skritch skritch. Willa turned. Roshni was pacing toward her, bobbing her head excitedly.

"Hello, Roshni." Willa smoothed the feathers on the bird's head, and Roshni nuzzled into her side, like a cat. Then the bird hopped over to the fireplace, dark and cold. She breathed on the log lying there and fanned it with her wings. There was a *fwoomp* and a flash of light as the log burst into flame.

Willa clapped her hands. "Bravo! I didn't know you could do that!"

Roshni hopped up and down, squawking. The log gave off a nice amount of heat, and Horace drew near to warm his hands. Willa made a mental note to gather more firewood, but as it turned out, that single log burned continuously until the spring, so there was no need for more.

The merry blaze transformed the parlour into the social centre of the house. Baz curled up happily on the braided rug in front of the fire while the others sat and chatted. Pots of tea, scones, and bowls of soup emerged periodically from the kitchen, courtesy of the dwarves, who slept there in hammocks strung from the ceiling. All in all, life at the house was pretty cozy.

No one had heard from Miss Trang since the snow started, but one afternoon she opened her bedroom door and started across the front hall toward the parlour. By now she was moving so slowly, it looked like the trip would take two or three days. Willa was worried about her. Her skin was weirdly shiny, you could see the faint shapes of scales in it, and her face seemed long and stretched, her eyes pulled back to the sides of her head, but nobody else took any notice of these changes. They simply stepped around her and carried on with their business.

One day Willa entered the house, stepped around the chandelier and promptly tripped over a large creature lying on the floor. Willa put her hand over her mouth to stifle a scream as she scrambled away from it. She sat for a moment, her back against the wall, staring at it in horror. It was about the size and length of a cow, but it was covered in scales and tapered to a long tail. Its head was tucked out of sight, and its body rose and fell gently as it slept on. Willa took a deep breath and stood on shaky legs. She tiptoed to the foot of the stairs and leaned over until she could see the creature's face. With a start she realized it was Miss Trang.

Miss Trang's face had stretched into a long snout, though her grey hair remained, still pulled into a bun at the back of her head. Hibernation had left her in semi-dragon, semi-human form. Willa found it creepy, but Horace said it was perfectly normal.

"Hibernation. Standard reptilian behaviour, nothing to be worried about. Happens every winter," he assured her.

Thankfully, Miss Trang wasn't full dragon size, but she was still as big as a sofa and formed a significant obstacle in the hall. The dwarves worked as a team to shift her closer to the wall so that Belle could get her wheelchair around her to enter the parlour. Everyone else walked around or clambered over her. Nothing, not even being stepped on, disturbed her sleep, and soon Miss Trang's inert figure on the floor became as familiar as a piece of furniture.

Chapter Four

Wintry shenanigans

The snow continued to fall, despite Horace's hand-wringing and embarrassment. As the town got used to the weather, people emerged from their houses to enjoy it, especially the neighbourhood kids. Tengu joined them, organizing the children into two armies, with fortifications and a large snowball arsenal.

Over the next week, Tengu tumbled in at dinner time soaked and frozen — feet numb, snow down his neck, his ears and nose red, and his eyes bright. The more he played with the kids, the younger he seemed to be. He'd sit on the comatose Miss Trang while Willa pulled his boots off, and entertain her with lively stories of the day's exploits.

"They call me the General," he told Willa proudly.

On Christmas Eve, after a big dinner, the dwarves served up eggnog and hot toddies in the parlour. Simple holly garlands were strung everywhere; they were even draped over the snoozing form of Miss Trang in the hallway, and a string of lights ran over her shoulders and across her snout. Willa was nervous about what she might think if she woke up, but she showed no signs of doing so.

Lit by the fire and candlelight, good cheer prevailed. Horace sang in his quavery voice about desert sands. Tengu shared some haiku he'd written. Mab floated in the middle of the room and sang a song of knights and ladies and courtly love. Emboldened by the rum toddies, Robert performed a soft-shoe dance routine, during which only one small end table was crushed. Baz didn't usually go in for performing, but tonight she climbed up on the back of the sofa, stood on one foot, and balanced three cups and saucers on her nose. The fact that they then fell and smashed only added to the fun. The dwarves took turns reciting stanzas of a very long and gruesome epic poem about warriors dismembering monsters and vice versa.

As the candles burned low, Belle ended the evening with a song, during which the whole group fell into a contented silence. The song was quite long, but the next day Willa could not for the life of her remember what it was about. She suspected Belle had put them into a trance.

As she walked home that gorgeously dark wintry night, Willa knew her mom and dad would have enjoyed the gathering, if they hadn't declined the invitation. Just as Belle would have turned down an invitation to Christmas dinner at Willa's house the next night, if Willa's mom hadn't already vetoed the very idea of inviting her. Belle and Mom would not forgive and forget, and get over their history.

At least Grandpa was there. Willa had always felt close to her grandpa, ever since she was a little girl spending blissful summers with him at the seashore. The sight of his sunbaked face, his bright blue eyes, and unruly mass of white hair brightened even her darkest day. As Willa and her parents laughed at Grandpa's stories over dinner, Willa reflected that she had, in effect, two warm, loving families, and that just made her feel lucky. Not only that, but as she watched her mom giving Grandpa a goodnight hug at the front door, she had a sudden flash of understanding about Mom's resentment toward Belle. Didn't Belle break up what close family she had, while Mom was just little? How would she herself feel if her mom just disappeared for no reason, leaving her and Dad on their own?

One day in early January, as Willa was scattering salt on the sidewalk to keep it from freezing over, Mrs. Norton came along, skittering a baby carriage over the bumpy ice. The Nortons had recently moved into a house across the street and a few doors down, and Willa knew they had a houseful of kids, from baby Everett all the way up to high school age. Mrs. Norton was a small woman with dishevelled hair and kindly, tired eyes. Willa had often helped her carry groceries into the house or round up her kids if she saw she was having trouble. Now Willa stepped up to help her steer the carriage on the ice. Inside, the baby gurgled happily.

"He's so smiley and quiet," said Willa as little Everett grinned up at her.

"Sure he is, *now!*" sighed Mrs. Norton. "But as soon as we get in the house he starts to fuss. And I've got all the laundry to do today!"

"If you like, I could look after him while you do your work," suggested Willa.

Mrs. Norton brightened at the thought. "You babysit?"

Willa glanced back at Eldritch Manor. "Yes, I do," she answered with a grin. "I've got lots of experience, though not with babies, exactly."

"Everett's very easy, apart from the fussing. He just gets restless and needs to be entertained. His brothers and sisters used to take turns minding him for me but they're all so busy lately…. Are you sure you don't mind?"

"Not at all! It's no problem. I'm here every day after school. Just bring him over whenever you need a break."

Mrs. Norton beamed. "Oh, Willa, you're a godsend! Thank you!" She handed over the diaper bag. "I'll come for him in a couple of hours!" she called over her shoulder as she hurried away.

Willa pushed Everett up and down the street for a while and then took him inside to warm up. As they entered the parlour, Mab looked up from her knitting.

"What's that?" she asked.

"Little Everett from down the street."

Mab flew closer to get a better look. This made Willa nervous. "Are you sure it's okay to let him see you?"

"Babies *always* see fairies," answered Mab. "We like

38

to visit very wee humans. When they get older, they forget all about us."

Everett's eyes went wide as saucers at the sight of her, and before she could react, his pudgy fist shot out and grabbed her.

"Everett, no! Let go!" exclaimed Willa. Mab gave him a sharp little zap. He flinched and opened his hand, though he didn't cry. Mab continued her inspection, circling at a safe distance.

"Everett. What kind of foolish name is that?"

"It's *his* name, Mab. I like it."

Mab leaned closer, staring into the baby's eyes, and her expression softened. "I shall call him Evling. Evling. Evvie wevvie bevvie boo! Wuvey dovey boy!"

Willa stared. This was a side of Mab she'd never seen before. Sulky she had seen, as well as haughty, outraged, spiteful, and wary. But coochie-cooing? Never!

Willa looked after Everett for a couple of hours, two or three times a week. Whenever Mab heard Everett's gurgly laughter, she came out to play peekaboo. She even nestled onto his pillow and sang lullabies. She had a knack for lulling him to sleep even in his crankiest moods, which made Willa uneasy.

"You're not magicking him to sleep, are you? I'd rather you didn't," she said one day, but Mab paid no attention.

The snow continued to fall. Mab refused to go outside, but the other fairies took to winter with glee. Fashioning bulky coats from moss and dandelion fuzz, they seemed impervious to the cold and devoted themselves to inventing new and ever more dangerous winter sports. They began sliding down snowbanks on a dead leaf, then took to leaping from high branches and plunging into the high drifts. Willa suggested once that Mab should go out and join them, but Mab was horrified at the thought of dressing up in a *snowsuit*. Willa admitted the bulky clothes made the fairies look like puffballs, but they were having such fun. Mab harumphed and disappeared into her wasp nest.

When the excitement of jumping into snowbanks wore off, Willa was shocked to catch them bumper-shining: flying up behind cars on the road, grabbing onto the back bumper, and hanging on for dear life as the car slid and skidded down the icy road. Willa called a halt to that one right away.

"What if you were seen? Or hurt? We wouldn't be able to find you, and ... and ..." This appeal had no effect on them, so Willa asked Mab to ban bumper-shining as "inherently unfairylike," and that stopped the practice.

"Goodness gracious," muttered Willa. "Why can't you just busy yourself with drawing those pretty frost patterns on the windows? And putting hoarfrost on the trees? I thought that's what fairies did all winter."

Sarah rolled her eyes at that. "*So* last century!"

January and February passed quite agreeably. Miss Trang snoozed on in the hallway, serving as a convenient bench for taking off one's boots. Everyone stayed cozy, and naps were frequent. Even the dwarves slowed in their work and spent the afternoons snoring in their hammocks. Willa walked to and from school in the soft whiteness of winter and did her homework in the quiet of the sleeping house.

The first of March dawned frosty and cold, with no sign of spring in sight.

"This is beyond my doing," Horace maintained. "Spring will come when it's ready, I suppose, and not a minute before."

It was another two weeks before Willa saw what she considered to be a real sign of spring. As she swept the snow from the porch, she had a sudden sensation of being watched. She looked up to see a small dark shape on the front walk: a brown hare, standing up on his hind legs and giving her a serious look. As Willa stared, he dropped down onto his four paws, but not before she caught a glimpse of gold at his breast.

Willa didn't know Roshni was around, but there was a sudden silent flash as the bird streaked down, and before the hare had time to react, Roshni had snatched him in her claws and lifted him into the air.

"Roshni!" hollered Willa. "No!"

Surprised, Roshni let go, and the rabbit dropped heavily to the ground. Willa ran up, not sure what to do. He lay on his back, panting heavily. Around his neck he wore a golden chain with a sun-shaped pendant.

Roshni landed nearby and paced, her head hung low. Willa positioned herself between the rabbit and the bird.

"I'm sorry, Roshni. I know you're a carnivore and everything, but this rabbit seems … different somehow. I mean, look! He's wearing a necklace."

At this the hare clapped a paw over it and gave her an indignant look. He leapt to his feet and bolted from the yard. As he paused in the street, looking back at her, his face broke into a wide, loopy grin. He took a wild leap into the air, twisting crazily, landed on four paws, and dashed from sight.

"Mad as a March hare," said Willa thoughtfully. It was an expression of her grandpa's that she'd never quite understood until this moment. Roshni nuzzled her beak under Willa's hand. "Oh it's all right, Roshni. You didn't know. That was no ordinary rabbit, so it's just as well you didn't eat him."

Willa gazed down the street and felt a warm breeze on her cheek. It did feel like spring all of a sudden, and she felt restless. She felt like leaping up in the air for no reason, just like the rabbit.

Mad as a March hare, she thought again, and took Roshni inside for a less bloodthirsty snack of raisin scones.

Chapter Five

An unexpected visitor

Willa soon forgot all about the strange rabbit. There was new excitement afoot, as the fairies had cooked up a very special event for the Spring Equinox: the first annual Eldritch Winter Games. It started out as the *Fairy* Winter Games, but Tengu and Robert declared there should be events for normal-sized individuals as well, and they joined the planning committee. Willa wasn't sure about the details of the games, but she was kept busy with fairy requests for fabric, bits of wood, scraps of plastic, paint, toothpicks, plastic wrap, tiny wheels, pillows, and all sorts of miscellaneous items. Excitement grew as the big day approached.

"This is going to be the biggest event of the year, next to Walpurgis Night," said Baz enthusiastically.

"What's Walpurgis Night?" asked Willa.

Baz squinted at her. "You're kidding, right?"

Willa shook her head. Baz rolled her eyes. "Humans are so clueless." And she wouldn't say another word about it.

The Winter Games fell on a cold, overcast Saturday. Willa came over in the morning, opening the front door and ducking reflexively under the chandelier before realizing it was suddenly a full foot above her head. Not just the chandelier — the ceiling itself was higher. The main hall seemed to be expanding upward.

Nothing surprises me about this place anymore, she thought with a smile, as she stepped around Miss Trang into the parlour. The house was quiet and empty, but she could hear hoots of laughter and cheering coming from the backyard. Willa peeked into the bowl on the mantle and was glad to see a healthy bundle of knitted scarf.

Good, Mab has been keeping up, she thought. She stood in the sunshine of the parlour, breathing in the silence, and had a sudden strange feeling that the peace would not last long. She sighed and went out into the yard.

The spectators were gathered: Belle in her wheelchair and the others in lawn chairs, everyone bundled up in mufflers and blankets. They were all looking down into the empty pool. At one end, a snowdrift sloped from the edge of the pool down to the bottom, where a slick of ice stretched to the opposite end of the pool. Here the fairies were skating, an entrancing sight as they swooped and twirled about. All was quiet at the moment save for the thin sounds of fairy fiddling and the scrape of skate blades on ice. The music and skaters swept to a dramatic finish, and the audience erupted in applause. Then followed an awkward moment as the judges couldn't agree on a winner. There was an argument over whether the best leap of the competition — Honeycup's jaw-dropping 3,240-degree rotation in mid-air, nine complete turns — had been aided by wing flaps, and whether or not that should be allowed. The spectators chimed in with their opinions, and finally Honeycup's jump was allowed and she received her gold medal.

Next was a thrilling mouse-sled race along a sharply curving course cut through the woods. The tiny animals threw themselves into the race with abandon; behind them the sleds bounced and crashed along, the fairies hanging on for dear life. At every corner, a fairy or two was flung right off, to the delight of the crowd. Every mouse completed the race, but the only fairy still on board at the finish line was plucky little Bergamot, so she was declared the winner.

A target had been painted on the stable wall for the Sharp Things Target Shoot. This event was, of course, Tengu's brainchild. The object was to hurl any sharp object at the target from the other side of the yard. Tengu, Robert, Baz, and four of the dwarves competed, though they were too impatient to properly wait their turn, so there was a steady, terrifying volley of darts, knives, forks, axes, ninja stars, swords, picks, arrows, and corkscrews flying across the yard in the general direction of the stable. All spectators fled the scene, preferring to watch from the safety of the kitchen window. When the competitors ran out of things to throw, the stable wall was such a scarred mess that no clear winner could be determined, despite much grumbling from those involved.

Willa moved with the others back to the pool for the bobsled race. She saw Horace gazing up at the sky and looked up to see the clouds bubbling and breaking up, slipping away at great speeds to reveal clear blue sky.

"That's weird," muttered Willa, taking her place poolside.

Eight bobsleds, carved from smooth driftwood and each holding three fairies in walnut shell helmets, lined the pool's edge, at the top of the snowdrift that sloped down to the bottom of the pool.

Sarah flew around searching for a good vantage point, finally settling onto Willa's shoulder. Willa eyed the racers with concern.

"Are they all going at once? I thought bobsleds usually went one at a time."

"Oh, this way is quicker," said Sarah. "And more exciting."

"What happens when they hit the ice at the bottom? Has anyone tested this course?" Willa asked nervously.

"I have no idea!" Sarah grinned.

When all the teams were in place, Mab, wrapped luxuriously in a robe that looked suspiciously like dryer lint, stepped up to call the start.

"On your mark, get set, GO!" Thrusting her finger into the sky, Mab shot a spray of sparks that snapped and popped overhead as the bobsleds plummeted down the icy slope. An excited cheer went up. A sudden warm breeze tickled around Willa's ears and neck, and as she watched, the ice surface at the bottom of the run glistened and shone, melting instantly. The carefully groomed slope began to run with water, and the bobsledders found themselves riding a river. Every time they banked for a turn, a spray of water went up. It was looking more like a water skiing competition than a bobsled race, and they hit the bottom with a huge splash. The bobsleds sank immediately, and sputtering fairies staggered out of the water, throwing off their helmets in disgust.

The crowd hushed and looked around in surprise. Snowbanks were shrinking away. Great clumps of snow fell from the trees, splattering onto the ground, and there was a sudden chitter of birdsong. Above them the last wisps of cloud slipped out of sight, leaving nothing but bright blue sky. Squinting in the sunshine, Willa turned questioningly to Belle, who shrugged. Horace, too, was speechless.

Sarah let out a gasp. Willa turned to see two large brown hares sitting at the corner of the house. They were identical to the one she had seen before, and they wore the same golden sun pendants.

The air grew warmer still. Everyone stared as the hares stepped aside to make way for four more hares carrying two long poles that supported a fairy-sized carriage, ornately carved in gold. They were followed by a dozen fairies walking behind. The Eldritch fairies, all females, were very woodsy, with garments roughly fashioned from leaves, twigs, and moss. This group, on the other hand, was made up entirely of male fairies, all in glittering medieval dress, and dripping with jewels.

The rabbits set the carriage on the ground, and they and the fairies all bowed low as a curtain drew aside and a glittering figure stepped out of the carriage.

It was a fairy. His long golden hair flowed in the warm breeze as he revealed his noble profile. He was brilliantly attired in yellow silk, with precious gems sparkling at his throat, and he held a fresh green fiddlehead staff. He seemed to glow from within. The noble figure stepped forward, leaving green, grassy footprints in the snow. He paused at the edge of the pool.

"Hello, Mab," he cooed.

All heads turned from the golden apparition to the other end of the pool, to Mab in her dryer lint cloak. She was scowling.

"Hello … *Oberon*," she hissed.

"I love your outfit," he crooned. "It brings out the grey in your hair."

Mab flung a fireball at him, but with a scooping motion Oberon countered it with a column of water from the melted puddle below. As the fireball hit it, both fire and water arched back and around. The shape of a heart hung in the air, half fire and half water. There was a smattering of applause as it slowly disintegrated and fell away.

With a loving look, Oberon held out his arms. "Dearest Mab!"

Silence. Willa held her breath, as did everyone else. Mab looked back coldly, not answering.

Willa heard Sarah whisper in her ear, "Isn't he dreamy?"

"Who is he?" Willa asked.

"Just the King of the Fairies, that's all," sighed Sarah. "*Mab's husband!*"

Chapter Six

The course of true love never did run smooth

"I didn't know Mab was married!" Willa exclaimed. "She never mentioned him before!"

Belle made a face. "Can't say as I blame her for not talking about that bubblehead."

They were sitting on the front porch. Tengu sat on the steps, his head in his hands as he watched the snow disappear. The sun beat down, and streams of water sparkled in the street. Willa took off her coat. "Where has he been?"

Belle let out a sudden laugh. "He's been everywhere … looking for her!"

"She ran away?"

"She decided to live elsewhere and left no forwarding address."

Willa gave Belle a sidelong glance before continuing. "I'm guessing they had a fight." An easy assumption to make, judging by Mab's reaction, and the fact that she refused to come out of her wasp nest to talk to him, no matter how lovey-dovey he acted. "He's still trying to talk her into coming out. Do you know why she's mad at him?"

"Who knows. They've been married for six hundred years, about five hundred of which they've spent bickering over one thing or another. I heard the latest argument was over a changeling...." Belle suddenly turned to Tengu. "Oh, stop your whimpering! It's driving me batty!"

"Beautiful snow! Gone! Gone forever!" he groaned.

"Tengu! It'll come back next winter! It always does!" Willa pointed out.

Tengu shook his head gloomily, and with one last heart-wrenching sigh, he shuffled into the house. Just then a group of fairies flew around the corner, chattering excitedly to each other.

"That hair! Did you see his hair?"

"And those eyes!"

"Gorgeous!"

"I know, right?"

Belle snorted, and the fairies finally noticed them there. They floated back the way they came, disappearing around the corner in a tinkle of laughter.

Belle rolled her eyes. "Fairies are idiots."

As Willa rolled Belle's chair inside, she was startled by a whoosh of wings in her face. Roshni was flapping awkwardly around the hall, landing finally on the chandelier, which swung crazily under her weight.

"Roshni! What's wrong?"

Horace came out of the parlour, stepping around Miss Trang. "There is some concern about the welfare of the rabbits with Roshni around. Apparently there was an incident?" He raised a questioning eyebrow.

"Oh," answered Willa, remembering. "About a week ago Roshni kind of ... picked one of them up. But she dropped him, and he was okay! It was an honest mistake. She thought he was just a regular bunny."

Horace hushed her, glancing nervously over his shoulder. "One does not call the Royal Guard of the King of the Fairies *bunnies!*"

"Rubbish!" Belle grumbled. "Bunnies are bunnies."

"Now, Belle," sighed Willa. "We should treat our guests with respect." She turned back to Horace. "Roshni won't go after them again, I promise."

On the chandelier, Roshni bobbed her head in agreement.

"You don't need to convince me — you need to convince *them*." Horace gestured back over his shoulder.

The parlour was crowded and noisy. Dwarves milled about, and fairies filled the air. Baz was wedged in with six rabbits on the sofa and did not look pleased. Robert sat in a corner throwing in his two cents every once in a while, and Tengu had his fingers in his ears.

"Oberon's crowd have lost no time in insulting the dwarves," reported Robert. "We're in for a donnybrook!"

Willa grimaced. The centuries-old animosity between fairies and dwarves had been extremely difficult to overcome, and she didn't want that feud to start up again. The dwarves glowered, the fairies tittered nervously, and everyone was talking at once.

Willa found a spot to park Belle and then made her way to the fireplace, trying not to step on anybody. The mantle was lined with fairies, the visiting fairies mingling with their own fairies, and all of them flirting and giggling.

Oberon floated beside the hanging wasp nest, speaking to Mab inside.

"Let me in, dearest doll," he crooned, smoothing his locks. "I yearn tragically for your love, my creampuff."

Mab responded with something unrepeatable.

Over Willa's head there was a sudden rush of air as Roshni swooped into the room. Shrieks went up from the visiting fairies.

"Savage monster! You shall taste my blade!" Oberon bellowed, drawing his sword from its jewelled sheath.

Roshni landed on Willa's head, and she staggered under the weight. "She's not a savage monster!" she protested, but Oberon charged at the bird, swinging his sword. There were screams, and fainting fairies littered the mantle. Willa threw up her hands to protect her face from the sword thrusts, as Oberon seemed more concerned with putting on a good show than aiming carefully. The rabbits hopped off the sofa and circled them. Roshni launched from Willa's head, sending her stumbling into rabbits, who in turn stumbled into dwarves. There was a lot of shouting.

Roshni flapped out into the hall. As Willa struggled to regain her balance, she saw Mab peeking out at the mayhem. Oberon flew after Roshni, but just then a crocheted pillow sailed through the air, taking him out completely. Cushion and fairy king crashed into the wall and dropped out of sight behind the sofa.

"Bravo!" cheered Robert, and Tengu took a bow.

The fairies who hadn't fainted before fainted now, and the rabbits drew their swords.

"Wait! Hold on!" yelped Willa, but she was cut off by a roar and a burst of flames overhead. Everyone fell into a shocked silence.

A large, scowling figure leaned in the doorway, smoke still curling from her nostrils.

"Can you keep it down?" snapped Miss Trang. "I'm trying to sleep here!"

Willa started to fill her in on recent events, but Miss Trang was not interested in anything other than going back to sleep and shuffled wearily into her room, slamming the door behind her.

Everyone seemed to regain their senses after this. The rabbits put away their weapons and the parlour was tidied up. Oberon was rescued from behind the sofa. He was sneezing from the dust and trying to ignore Mab's laughter. Willa attempted to convince him that Roshni was not a threat to anyone, but Oberon was so peeved and the rabbits looked so stern that she finally agreed the bird would be kept far away from the visitors. She dug out the birdcage, but Roshni wouldn't go near it. After further consultation, Fjalarr suggested putting Roshni in the attic.

"The attic?" asked Willa, confused. "You mean the second floor?"

"No, we'll whip up an attic right away, before we do the second and third floors."

That one left Willa scratching her head, but a couple of days later Fjalarr delivered on his promise. Willa and Roshni joined him up on top of the finished first floor, where they found a rope tied to a crossbeam with the other end extending up into a small white cloud. Fjalarr pulled the rope, and down from the cloud descended the attic: a small square room with a window in each of its four sides, floating in the air like a balloon.

Willa gasped in astonishment.

"The wind pushes it around a little, but it's perfectly safe," explained Fjalarr as he drew the room down to them. Willa opened the door and set Roshni inside before climbing in herself.

The attic was empty save for a fixed wooden perch in the centre of the room. Roshni hopped onto it and looked around approvingly. The windows provided a breathtaking view of the town and the ocean beyond.

"It's absolutely amazing," exclaimed Willa, jumping back down to join the dwarf and nervously scanning the street. "But we'd better keep it out of sight."

Fjalarr let go of the rope, and the attic bobbed up again, disappearing into the cloud.

"That's why we made the cloud." He gazed up at it in admiration. "Especially puffy, that is. Fine craftsmanship."

"Oh yes, it's really lovely," admitted Willa, though deep down she thought it still looked pretty suspicious floating there all by itself.

Chapter Seven

In which everyone loses their minds

When Willa entered the house the next day, she found what looked like a long, crumpled piece of mottled tissue paper lying in the hall.

"What *is* this?" She leaned down for a closer look. Baz appeared at her elbow, very interested.

"Ooh, I can't believe she just left it here!" Baz lifted it carefully and began rolling it up.

"Who?"

"Miss Trang."

"I thought she was still sleeping."

"She was up this morning, just long enough to get a cup of tea …" Baz held up the roll. "And shed this."

Willa recoiled. "Wait, that's her *skin?* Eww!"

Baz rolled her eyes. "Dragons shed their skin. Fact of life, get over it." She gave the rolled bundle a little pat. "She was so sleepy that she forgot to burn it. Dragons always burn their skin after shedding it."

"Why?"

"To keep it from falling into the wrong hands. There's

a lot of magic in this baby, and if the wrong person picked it up …" Baz shook her head. "Let's just say it would not be a good thing. I'll take very good care of this." Baz hurried off down the hall with her treasure cradled in her arms, muttering excitedly. "And only thirty-eight days until Walpurgis Night…"

"What is Walpurgis Night?" Willa called after her but got no answer.

Because Mab had laughed at him during the parlour mishap, Oberon now refused to speak to her. All day long, fairies flew back and forth between the wasp nest and the carriage on the mantle, delivering grievances and insults between husband and wife. As the squabble became more pronounced, the weather grew gloomier. Dark clouds hung low in the sky, blocking the especially puffy attic cloud from sight, to Willa's great relief.

One afternoon, Willa and Belle were sitting in the parlour with Everett in his carriage. Mab was floating over him, jabbering away in baby talk, and Oberon flew over to take a look. He had never shown any interest in the baby before, and as he leaned in at Mab's elbow, she turned on him in a fury.

"What do you want?"

"I'm just looking," Oberon huffed.

"Well, I saw him first!" spat Mab. "Back off!" The two fairies glared at each other, forehead to forehead, eyeball to eyeball.

"How dare you—" started Oberon.

"How dare *I*?" sputtered Mab, so angry that sparks shot out of her hair. Oberon jumped back.

"Watch it, sweetie. You never could control your temper."

With a growl, Mab flew at him, shooting deep red sparks out on all sides. Oberon returned the fire, and the two fairies zapped wildly at each other, hovering in the centre of the room about two feet apart.

"Not so close to the baby!" shouted Willa, wheeling him out of range of the fireworks. Everett clapped his hands and giggled.

A *crash* of thunder drew Willa's attention to the window. Outside, the dark clouds flashed with lightning. Willa looked thoughtfully from the clouds to the fairies and back again.

"Belle," she whispered, "Do you suppose…"

Just then Oberon shot a very large yellow bolt at Mab. There was a blinding flash outside at the exact same moment.

Willa clutched Belle's arm. "They're doing it, aren't they? They're making it storm!"

"I wouldn't doubt it. Troublemakers."

Flashes ricocheted around the room. One hit the wasp nest and burned a small hole in it. Mab let out a shriek and flew over to blow out the sparks. Oberon began to follow, but Willa thrust a tea tray between him and the nest and corralled him back to his carriage.

"Time out! Time out!"

Oberon harumphed but withdrew inside and pulled the curtain shut. Willa breathed a sigh of relief. Outside, the lightning died away and rain poured down in sheets.

On the mantle, Willa caught sight of the knitting bowl, which had been shoved back behind Oberon's carriage. She pulled it closer and peeked inside. A mere inch or two of scarf remained in the bottom of the bowl. As Willa stared, the stitches unravelled … one … by one … by one …

"Mab! Mab!" Willa grabbed the bowl. "The knitting! Don't forget to keep knitting!"

Mab sat in the doorway of the wasp nest, angrily cracking her knuckles. At the sight of the scarf, she shook her head. "Don't feel like it," she growled.

"But Mab!" pleaded Willa. "You *have* to! It's nearly all gone!"

The fairy snarled and retreated into the nest, slamming the door. Willa turned and gave Belle a wide-eyed look.

"How can we keep her knitting?"

"You can't force Mab to do anything she doesn't want to do," answered Belle.

"Yes, but if the scarf runs out …" Willa's words died away. If the scarf ran out, the house, with them in it, would drop out of time. They'd drop right out of the human world, and they'd be lost in that awful grey void again. She shivered.

"Sarah!" she yelped. The little fairy jumped up from where she was sitting in the hibiscus with one of Oberon's minstrels, a fair-haired fellow with a lute.

"Is there anyone else who can knit?" Willa asked. "Any other fairy, I mean? It's too small for normal sized fingers. Sarah … Sarah?"

Sarah was peeking over her shoulder, blowing kisses at the lute player. Willa snapped her fingers in front of her face. "Earth to Sarah!"

Sarah blinked. "Sorry, um … this is Hubert. Have you heard him play the lute? He's so talented—"

"I haven't heard him, and I don't want to!" snapped Willa, and then she dropped her voice. "I'm getting a little tired of Oberon and his fairies. They've cast a spell over all of you."

Sarah straightened and gripped her clipboard. "All I said was that he could play the lute," she muttered.

"Just go and see if you can find a fairy who can knit. Please?"

Belle shook her head as Sarah flew off. "You can't depend on fairies. They've got the attention span of addled gnats. All it would take is a smile from King Hairdo and they'd forget all about knitting."

"Are you telling me *Mab* is the most responsible one of the lot?" marvelled Willa. "We're in more trouble than I thought." She began to pace. "They weren't always this useless. What's come over everybody?"

Belle chuckled. "Love is in the air…."

There was a knock on the door. Willa started for the front hall, still muttering. "Well, it's making them loopy. They've all lost their minds!"

She swung the door open and found herself staring into the bluest eyes she'd ever seen in her life.

"Hi. You must be Willa? I'm Jake."

He was a tall boy, and she stared up at him, not knowing what to say. There was an awkward silence. He blushed and ran his fingers through his longish hair.

"I'm Everett's brother. I came to pick him up."

"Oh! Oh, yes," Willa stammered. "Let me get him."
The brother! she thought. *The one in high school. I didn't know he was so … tall.*

She hurried into the parlour and looked around quickly to make sure there was no weirdness on display. All the fairies had ducked out of sight. As she gathered Everett's blankie and toys, she saw Jake eyeing the smouldering wasp nest in the corner, but he didn't comment.

After she had handed Everett in his carriage over to the bluest eyes in the world, Willa stood in the doorway watching them disappear down the street. Behind her, Belle chuckled.

"What were you saying just now? Who's lost their minds?"

Willa blushed but didn't answer.

Chapter Eight

A glitch in time

Willa returned to the parlour. *Okay. Time to focus.* She went to the mantle and pulled out the tiny bit of scarf, which was slowly disappearing before her eyes.

Horace wandered in, and his eyes widened at the sight of it. "Oh dear."

Sarah buzzed into the room and lit on the back of the sofa, out of breath. "I've been all through the woods and talked to every single one of our fairies."

"And?" asked Willa.

"No volunteers."

Willa groaned. "Don't they know how serious this is?"

Sarah shrugged. "I could try Oberon's fairies. Maybe Hubert…?" She gazed over at her friend on the mantle.

Horace made a face. Belle snorted. "Not a good idea. I wouldn't trust them."

Willa looked at her with wild eyes. "But we haven't got much time left … Sarah!"

Sarah was batting her eyes at Hubert. Willa waved the last inch of scarf in front of her face. "Sarah! Focus!

We need a knitter! Mab won't do it, and only tiny hands can handle this. I tried once, but my stitches made time really clunky." Willa's gaze fell to Sarah's hands clasped around the clipboard. Sarah yelped and hid her hands behind her back.

"I'm a terrible knitter!" she squealed.

"*You know how to knit?*" Willa fought to stay calm. "Sarah, please help us. You can do this. You're clever. If this scarf runs out we drop into nothingness, the void! No outside world … no sun, no stars, no … groceries! Please, Sarah! Pleeease?"

Sarah blushed. "You really think I'm clever?"

"Of course!" Willa dropped her voice to a whisper. "Who else could keep Mab in line?"

"I suppose I could give it a try." Sarah climbed into the knitting bowl and set to work. None too soon, as the knitting had dwindled to only two rows by the time she got started. Willa breathed a little easier to see her concentrating on her work and watched over her shoulder until Sarah looked up in irritation. "Do you mind?"

"Sorry. I'll give you some space." Willa wandered out into the hall. She opened the front door and stared out at the pouring rain. She frowned, thinking of their bright, sunny winter months, and of the peace and calm they'd been enjoying. *Everything was just perfect until Oberon showed up!*

Willa shut the door, turned, and let out a surprised yelp at the sight of a solemn rabbit standing in the hall watching her. It didn't budge as she edged back into the parlour. *Those bunnies are creeping me out,* she thought.

Willa couldn't help herself; she peeked into the bowl again. Sarah had finished a few rows, but the stitches were bumpy and uneven, and there were two small holes where she'd dropped stitches.

"Um, it's a good start," said Willa.

"I'm doing my best," said Sarah crossly. "I may be clever, but that doesn't make me handy, you know."

Horace was now at her side. Willa showed him the scarf. "Those holes, do you think they'll affect time at all?"

Horace was nodding thoughtfully. "Perhaps. We won't have long to find out."

It was true. The unravelling had almost reached the first little gap. Horace walked to the window, and Willa followed.

They stared out at the rain. Suddenly Horace pointed. "There it is."

A silvery, shimmering blob moved down the road, sometimes along the ground, sometimes drifting up to float through the air. It was about the size of a car and wobbled unsteadily, like a bubble.

"What is it?" breathed Willa.

"A hole in time."

As it lurched along, a dark shape tumbled out of it into the street.

"And what's that?" asked Willa.

"This hole is simply one end of a corridor from another time. Objects sometimes get caught in these corridors and fall out the other end," said Horace. "Tengu, would you mind checking it out?"

Willa heard the front door slam, and Tengu trotted outside. He jumped out of the way of the silver bubble as it veered off the roadway, moved up their front walk, and poured across the parlour window like silver paint.

A bright white glow passed down the main hallway, sweeping to the back of the house. Willa, Belle, and Horace stared at each other in the weird, glistening light, then everything returned to normal.

"It's gone right through the house," said Horace. Willa dashed to the window at the end of the hall and looked out into the backyard. She saw the bubble shimmy across the grass and slip into the pool. She waited, but it didn't emerge again.

"It's in the pool!" she hollered. The front door slammed shut, and she went to meet Tengu in the hall. He held up a large, rough wooden bucket.

"It was just a bucket that fell out. Nice one, though."

There was a rumbling sound, and they jumped back as the trapdoor to the basement opened. Robert came thundering up, followed by a few dwarves.

"What the blazes just happened? We were in the middle of a friendly game of cards and I was just about to win the pot when it disappeared into some kind of … of …"

"Time hole," said Horace. "It was a time hole."

"Well, it's a damn nuisance!" growled Robert. "I lost half a deck of cards *and* a goodly pile of dwarf gold!"

Sarah looked at them all, her eyes as big as saucers. "Did I do that?" she squeaked. "All I did was drop a stitch!"

"Mab! Get out here and start knitting!" Willa barked at the wasp nest. "NOW!"

Mab emerged, her lips pursed, but she gave no argument. She flew over to the bowl, took the knitting from Sarah, and got to work. Willa glanced quickly at the scarf. "There's one more coming up."

Everyone crowded around the window. Willa heard the front door open and saw Tengu saunter out to the road again.

"There it is!" rasped Horace, pointing.

"Good heavens, look at it!" muttered Belle.

It was bigger, as tall as a tree, floating along above the rooftops. As it approached, it suddenly swooped to the ground. Willa caught a glimpse of a dark shape dropping from it, and Tengu running to catch it.

"Brace yourselves!" shouted Horace as the bubble hit the house. The parlour was suffused with blinding light. There was a loud *whoosh* of wind in Willa's ears, and a deathly chill passed through her. She groped her way past Robert and stumbled down the hall to the rear window.

The silvery bubble collapsed and filled the yard like a shining flood. Then it began draining away. Down and down it went, spiralling away and disappearing into the pool.

Silence.

"Everything all right?" Horace joined her at the window.

"The time holes both went into the pool," said Willa. "What does that mean?"

Horace thought for a moment. "I'm not sure. Let's take a look."

They went outside, and Willa shone her flashlight into the pool. There was about a foot of rainwater down there, and she could see two silver bubbles resting on the bottom of the pool like beads of mercury — one small and one large.

"How odd," said Horace, frowning. "Time holes usually disappear after just a few moments. They're extremely unstable."

Horace fetched a broom and poked one of the bubbles with the handle. There was a sudden *whoosh*, and the broom was sucked out of his hand, disappearing into the bubble, which wavered for a moment and was still again.

"Hmm," he said.

"They both headed straight for the pool," said Willa. "Like they were drawn to it."

Horace stood for a while in thought. "A location-specific phenomenon. This pool must be some kind of time wrinkle."

Willa looked at him weakly. "I'm not even going to pretend to understand what you're talking about."

Horace nodded, smiling. "That's probably best."

As they entered the front hall, Tengu was just slipping into his room.

"What fell out of that one?" asked Willa.

Tengu peeked out again. "Nothing much. Sticks, dead branches. Well, I'm beat, goodnight!" And with a quick wave he disappeared into his room.

Horace was already in the parlour. A large boot had suddenly appeared on the coffee table, but there was no evidence of anything else falling out of the time hole. Eikinskjaldi came out of the kitchen to report they'd lost a toaster in the first time hole and a pot-scrubber in the second.

"That's all? Good!" replied Willa, but the dwarf was really bummed.

"It was an outstanding toaster," he sighed.

Willa collapsed on the sofa. "Mab, we need to find you a backup knitter. Someone who doesn't drop stitches. No offense, Sarah."

Sarah didn't appear to have heard her; she was back in the hibiscus plant with her lute player. Willa looked up at Mab, who was eyeing her warily.

"It would take some of the pressure off you, Mab. You must get tired of knitting."

Mab considered, nodding. "I do, actually."

"It's got to be someone who can do the same fine work. Do you think any of the other fairies…?"

Mab shook her head quickly, rolling her eyes.

"Who else is there?" Willa asked helplessly.

"We might put out a general advertisement among all the Little People," Mab answered. "Sarah, see to it at once!" She turned, looking around the room. "Sarah!"

Sarah gave Hubert a quick peck on the cheek before flying up. "Yes, Your Extravagancy?"

Mab gave her quick instructions, and Sarah flew off. Mab turned back to Willa. "We'll find someone right away. Goodnight!" She started for her wasp nest.

Willa cleared her throat. "Um, Mab? Could you knit a few more rows before you go to sleep? Just to get us through the night?"

Mab scowled, but she plunked herself in the bowl and got to work.

At home that night, Willa fell wearily into bed. The sound of the wind and rain in the trees carried her off to sleep, and she dreamed of an endless sea of green. The air was filled with the whisper of leaves, but underneath was an insistent, scratchy, skittering sound, which continued through the night.

Chapter Nine

Eight legs to the rescue

Mab was right. It only took one day to find a knitter. When Willa arrived at the house after school the next day, Sarah fluttered up in a tizzy.

"It's … we've … I can't —" She gasped.

"Hold on, calm down. What happened?"

Sarah took a deep breath, then squealed, "New knitter!"

"Good!" Willa kicked her boots off and entered the parlour. More fairies, including Oberon's entourage, swarmed around her.

"Simply unacceptable!"

"Outrageous!"

"It can't be allowed!" they shrieked.

Pressing her hands over her ears, Willa pushed her way through the mob. "Let me through, please!"

The rabbits were in a semicircle facing the bowl on the mantle, their swords drawn. Willa could see Oberon peeking out of his carriage, clearly terrified.

"It'll kill us all!" he yelped before disappearing inside. The rabbits stepped aside to allow Willa through. Mab stood next to the knitting bowl, her arms crossed, clearly delighted with the uproar.

"You found someone?" asked Willa. Mab nodded and gestured grandly to the bowl. The fairies fell silent as Willa rose up on her tiptoes to peek inside. She found herself face to face with a massive, hairy black spider.

"Hello darlin'," it purred.

"Aaahh!" Willa jumped back. "*That's* your new knitter?"

"Yes," crowed Mab. "Her name is Tabitha, and she comes with excellent references. She won the Woodland Textile Expo eight times in a row." Willa looked in at the spider again. She couldn't believe how big she was. Her body was as large as Willa's fist, and she was mostly black, though now Willa noticed patches of white hair on her legs, which were neatly folded in front of her. She had enormous, shiny black discs for eyes: two big ones in the centre and two smaller ones to the sides.

"So nice to meet you," said Tabitha softly.

"Hello. I'm Willa."

"Tabitha can spin, sew, weave, embroider, knit, darn, and crochet," announced Mab. "She knows a thousand different stitches!"

"Oh now, miss, you're embarrassing me," Tabitha protested, ducking her head shyly.

"But it's all true!" said Mab proudly. "Go on, show her."

Without taking her large, unblinking eyes off Willa, Tabitha picked up the ball of yarn, tossed it deftly from leg to leg, and began to knit. Instead of needles, she used her legs, which flashed back and forth with machine-like precision. Yarn loops appeared and slipped through each other at lightning speed, forming row after effortless row. Willa stared in amazement.

Mab sighed happily. "Isn't she magnificent?"

Tabitha modestly dropped her gaze, and the fairies started up again with their complaints, clustering behind Willa for protection.

"She'll catch us in a web!"

"She'll eat us!"

"You can't let her stay!"

Willa addressed the spider firmly. "Your work is wonderful, but you can only stay if you promise not to harm the fairies."

Tabitha's main eyes widened and she let out a little gasp. "I wouldn't dream of it! Why, I wouldn't hurt a fly!"

"Which is why the fairies will supply her meals," said Mab. "So she doesn't have to hunt for food." There was a buzz of protest from the fairies, but Mab silenced them with an imperious glare.

Willa turned back to Tabitha. "Has Mab told you how important this scarf is?"

"Yes, and I promise to be hardworking, discreet, and reliable." The spider's entire face curved into a smile. "You can count on me, darlin.'"

Willa smiled back. An industrious spider would definitely be a step up from Mab or any of her flighty subjects. And she certainly seemed qualified — her knitting was rapid, smooth, and perfect. Not a single dropped stitch.

"Welcome to Eldritch Manor, Tabitha," said Willa.

"Thank you," answered the spider.

As Willa turned away, she saw Baz gazing at the spider with a strange, glazed look in her eye.

"Baz! Tabitha is not a snack! Leave her alone, all right?"

"Who, me? Why, I wouldn't hurt a fly," purred Baz, retreating to the sofa.

Sarah and the other fairies were still a bit frightened of Tabitha, but when they brought her the dead flies they'd collected from around the house, she thanked them so politely that they were soon won over. The knitting bowl was removed from the mantle and hung below Mab's nest. Tabitha could work in peace there, out of Baz's reach, and Mab gained an immense watch-spider outside her door. Tabitha's presence certainly kept Oberon away, as he was absolutely terrified of the spider. Thus deprived of access to his lady-love, Oberon spent his time glumly digging into the mantle with his bejewelled sword, carving little hearts with "O+M" in the centre.

Willa was not particularly fond of Oberon, but this was just too pathetic to bear. And as pleased as she was with Tabitha, Mab became increasingly distracted and moody. More than once Willa caught her gazing sadly in Oberon's direction, though she always looked away if he chanced to look back.

It didn't much matter to Willa if they ever made up again, but she suspected that if they resolved their differences, the rain might stop and the blessed sun appear again. Every day was the same dark, dreary, soggy mess, and it was getting Willa down.

"Go and talk to him!" she said to Mab, who harumphed and slammed her door.

"Go and talk to her!" she said to Oberon. He was lying face down on the mantle and did not respond.

"They're acting like teenagers," she complained to Belle, who was sitting at the window staring out at the backyard.

"They *are* teenagers. Eight-hundred-year-old teenagers," Belle observed. "You can't make a fairy do anything they don't want to do, and that includes growing up." She pointed out the window. "This is much more interesting than idiot fairies. Take a look at *that!*"

Willa squinted out the window at the rain and fog. "I don't see anything."

"The pool!" hissed Belle. "Look at the pool! It's filling up!"

The rain was, indeed, slowly filling the pool, which was now half full of dark green water.

"Looks gross."

"Nonsense!" Belle rubbed her hands gleefully. "It's lovely! Let's go out for a closer look!"

Willa found an umbrella and wheeled Belle outside. They stared down at the water, their reflections scattered by raindrops. Strands of algae floated on the surface and streaked the sides of the pool.

Willa made a face. "There's all kinds of goo growing in there."

"It's not that bad. You'll see when we swim in it."

"Ew! No way."

"You'll see."

"No, I won't. I'm not going in, ever, because I don't swim!" Willa explained, but Belle wasn't listening. Willa stared glumly at the pool. "That's where the time holes went, you know."

Willa could see silver at the bottom of the pool. She found a stick and pushed aside the muck on the surface, leaning down for a better look.

"They're still there," said Willa.

"What?"

"The time holes," replied Willa. "Horace said they usually disappear, but these ones haven't yet."

"Ooh!" Belle was growing more and more interested. "Time holes, eh? Pop through one of those and you could end up anywhere, any *time*...."

"Any time," said Willa thoughtfully. "Horace says this pool is a wrinkle in time."

"That's very likely. Remember the dinosaur?"

Willa nodded. In the summer, when they'd first discovered the pool hidden in the bushes and weeds, they'd also found a dinosaur and named her Dinah. She'd been hibernating in the pool for goodness knows how long. They took her to the ocean, and she was now swimming free somewhere, but they'd never figured out how she'd come to be curled up in a small backyard pool.

Willa stared down at the bubbles, fascinated. "Look there, see the smaller one? I think there's a teeny plant growing out of it." She looked up, but Belle was wheeling herself back to the house.

Darkling Green

That night Willa dreamed she was sitting in the parlour at Eldritch Manor, but everything was green, the floor, the walls, the furniture, everything, and as she sat there the room began to twist and stretch. She shouted, but her voice was lost in the deafening noise of cracking wood. The room burst upward, growing like the magic beanstalk in the fairy tale. Willa tried to run out of the room, but her feet were rooted to the floor, and she felt herself pulled and stretched, twisting and twining upward with the rest of the house, until everything fell into a confused blur and she woke up.

Chapter Ten

In which spring is sprung

"I'll never understand why people prefer spring to winter! It's wretched!" exclaimed Tengu the next day, balancing on one foot while he poured water out of his left boot. Willa, huddled under her umbrella, was inclined to agree. The backyard was a sodden mess of mud and leaves. Above them, dark clouds crowded the sky, and the rain poured down. Willa leaned back to look up at the house. The little attic cloud still hung above the place, white against the dark sky. The white beams for the second floor were advancing steadily; the entire storey was now sketched out in framework.

"I think the rain is helping the house grow," said Willa. "But I still wish it would stop."

"The house isn't the only thing that's growing," muttered Tengu, joining her beside the pool. He was right. The algae had continued its spread up the sides of the pool, and where it emerged from the water, wrapping over the lip of the pool, it was growing longer and shaggier. Willa crouched down and poked it with her finger.

"It's so thick, it's turning into moss. Look, it's like a sponge." She poked it again, and water ran out. Peering through the slime, Willa could just make out the silver bubbles on the bottom of the pool.

"Still there," she said.

"What's still there?" Tengu asked.

"The time holes." Willa pointed. "And see that plant growing out of the small one? It was only a tiny twig yesterday!" The green shoot now stretched to the wall of the pool and had climbed halfway up.

Willa and Tengu wandered into the trees. Everywhere they looked, new sprouts were pushing up through the dead leaves.

"Last week everything was covered with snow, and now it's so green! How could all this happen so quickly?" marvelled Willa.

"Oberon and his bunch," Tengu answered simply. "They've thrown things out of whack."

"You can say that again." Willa looked up at the dark sky. "I can't even tell what time it is, it's so dark." She checked her watch, which said four fifteen. "Darnit. My watch has stopped. It must be nearly six. I should be getting home for supper."

Inside the house, the clock in the hall had the same time as her watch: four fifteen. As did the parlour clock and Horace's pocket watch.

"It *can't* be four fifteen!" Willa exclaimed. She'd walked over from school, arriving just before four o'clock, and she'd sat for a cup of tea with Belle and then chatted with the dwarves a little before wandering around the yard.

Horace considered this. "The day *ha*s seemed to drag a little," he admitted with a yawn and wandered off into the hall.

Time behaving weirdly can mean only one thing, thought Willa, moving toward the wasp nest and the bowl beneath. She stood on a stool to look inside. Tabitha wasn't there, but Willa was glad to see a large mass of silvery scarf, so long it wound round and round the inside of the bowl, creating a cozy pillow.

"Nice!" murmured Willa. She gingerly lifted a fold of the scarf. It was exquisite. The stitches were so smooth and fine, she could barely see them. When she turned the scarf over in the light, she could see a pattern of vines and leaves running through it. She heard a small cough. Tabitha was on the floor beside the stool, staring up at her.

"Oh hello, Tabitha. I was just looking for you."

The spider didn't reply but scurried up the stool leg then up Willa's leg and side. Willa held her breath. Tabitha paused on her shoulder for a moment before leaping into the bowl.

"Your work is really beautiful," Willa said.

"Why thank you, darlin'. That means a lot to me." Tabitha smiled.

Willa paused, unsure about how to proceed. "I think, though, that your stitches are… quite a bit *smaller* than Mab's." The spider lifted her big, buggy eyes in shock.

"Are they? Oh dear, I am so sorry! I hadn't noticed!" Tabitha began circling the bowl anxiously. "I'll pull it all out and start again!"

"No, no!" protested Willa. "It's all right, it's just that time is moving a teensy bit slower. It's really no problem at all."

Tabitha hung her head and sniffled. Willa felt awful. "I'm sorry, I don't mean to criticize. You do lovely work. Absolutely gorgeous."

Tabitha answered in a quavery voice. "You are kind. I'll try to do better, I promise. It's just that the size of the stitches is determined by the size of the needles." Here she held up two legs. "I will do my very best to knit a little larger."

"Thank you, Tabitha. I really appreciate it. Sorry to interrupt!" Willa retreated and went to knock on Horace's door. He opened it, yawning.

"Hmm? Yes?"

"Horace, I forgot to tell you. The time holes are still there, in the pool. And," she dropped her voice to a whisper, "Tabitha is knitting with really small stitches. I think it's making time slow down."

"At least she isn't dropping stitches," he offered with a shrug and yawned again. "Oh my heavens, I need a nap. I feel like I haven't slept in days."

As Willa pulled on her coat, she looked out the window. Two kids were running past the house in super slow motion. A pigeon hung in the air in the middle of an excruciatingly slow wingflap, and rain drops oozed their way to the ground.

"The clocks match the time out there, which is slower than it is here," she said to herself, her brows furrowed in consternation. "So if I come in here for what feels like a few hours, it's really only a few minutes out there." She sighed. "At least that means I won't be late for supper."

Just then she caught sight of Jake Norton across the street on his way home. He strode along, his hair lifting and falling with each long-legged step — the slo-mo lending his movements a grace they probably wouldn't have had in normal time. Willa watched, mesmerized, until he disappeared slowly from sight. Then her thoughts were interrupted by a sound behind her. It was Tengu, emerging from his room with a large bowl in his hand.

"Hi, Tengu."

He nearly jumped out of his skin. "Ack! Willa, didn't see you there." He quickly shut the door behind him. "Just … getting a drink of water."

Willa looked at the bowl in his hand. Tengu looked at the bowl in his hand. "Couldn't find a glass," he stammered.

Willa shrugged and zipped up her coat. "Well, g'night. I'm going home." She hesitated, looking into the parlour, listening to the *flick flick flick flick* of Tabitha's knitting legs. "I wish I could stay and keep an eye on everything, though I'd need eyes in the back of my head for that."

Tengu grinned and snapped his fingers. "Leave it to me," he said, and hurried off down the hall.

Chapter Eleven

A turn for the worse

"Mmm. The water looks so inviting." Belle was gazing out the window at the pool again.

"You can't be serious," Willa replied. "It's more gruesome every day."

Indeed, the pool was almost full, but the water was like brown soup. Lumpy brown soup with a bubbly scum of algae covering the surface.

"Look again," said Belle. She had an odd tone in her voice, but she sounded deadly serious, so Willa looked again.

"Well? What do you see?" prodded Belle.

"Goo and slime."

"It doesn't make you want to go for a swim?"

"No!" Willa shivered.

"Come here, lean closer."

Willa did so, and Belle placed her hands on either side of Willa's head, just behind her ears. Willa looked into her eyes.

"You know what you are, don't you?"

Willa laughed. "*What* I am? I know *who* I am."

Belle fixed her with a steady stare, her hands resting lightly on Willa's head and her fingers probing her scalp. It was a weird sensation that reminded Willa of something. She pulled away, frowning.

Belle laughed. "You know you're not entirely human." Then Belle's voice sounded in Willa's head, though her mouth did not move.

You can send and receive messages with your mind, can't you?

Surprised, Willa nodded. How did Belle know? Horace must have told her. Belle's voice rang in her head again.

You are like me.

Uncomfortable, Willa stepped away from her. "Like you?" She gestured down to her legs. "I'm *not* a mermaid!"

Belle cocked her head slyly. "The tail isn't everything, you know. I went without mine for a time." She reached out and took Willa's hands in her own, grinning mischievously. "There's a little bit of mermaid in you, somewhere, and we're going to wake it up with a little *swim*! You're turning thirteen soon, right?"

"Day after tomorrow," Willa admitted. "I nearly forgot about it, I've been so busy."

"On what date?"

"April first."

"April Fools' Day!" exclaimed Belle gleefully. "Wonderful! Thirteen is a very significant age for mermaids. It's high time I undertook your training, and a birthday swim is how we begin…."

"I can't," Willa responded.

"You'll get over the slimy water."

Willa tried again. "But I really can't do it."

"The algae feels cool and lovely on the skin, you'll see. We'll just ease in and—"

"BELLE!" Willa exploded.

Belle blinked in surprise. Willa took a deep breath. "It's not because of the algae! I can't do it because I can't swim. At all."

"Oh, I can teach you."

There was a loud knock at the front door.

"Can somebody get that?" called Willa and turned back to Belle. "You don't understand. I don't want to learn."

Another loud knock.

"Someone get the door!" Back to Belle. "I *can't* learn. I'm … I'm …"

A final impatient knock at the front door made Willa jump. "Oh, for heaven's sake! Can't anybody else answer the door around here?"

Belle had turned away to gaze at the pool. Willa stomped to the front door and swung it open.

"Yes?" She froze.

An immense man covered in tattoos filled the doorway.

"Does Tengu live here?" he asked.

"Argus!" Tengu bounded past Willa and pumped the man's hand. "How are you, you big galoot?" Barely reaching the man's elbow, Tengu squinted up at him. "Less hair, I see. And more flab. Still working out?" He punched the man in the belly. The man didn't move a muscle.

"Sure, when I can," he answered. "You said you had a job for me?"

"We do," replied Tengu. "If you don't mind coming out of retirement for it."

The man smiled ruefully. "Being retired is all right for a hundred years or so, but after that it gets a little boring. I need something to do."

"Excellent," said Tengu. "Come in! Come in!"

The big man had to duck his head to get through the doorway. Tengu led him into the parlour, and Willa followed.

"This is Willa," announced Tengu.

The man bowed, giving Willa a view of the tattoos that covered his bald head. They were eyes, and one of them winked at her.

Willa gasped. Tengu chuckled. "Willa, meet my good friend Argus. You said you wanted someone to keep an — *eye* — on things, right? Well, Argus is the best man for the job. Check it out!" Tengu spun the big man around to reveal a dozen more eyes staring back at her.

"He's got eyes in the back of his head!" exclaimed Tengu.

"Wow," said Willa simply.

"That's not all," Tengu went on. "Roll up your sleeves, Argus."

Argus sighed wearily, but he took off his raincoat and rolled up his shirtsleeves. His arms were covered in eyes, real eyes, set into the skin. Each eye was looking around independently of the others; they were all gazing in different directions.

"How many are there?" Willa asked.

"A hundred. Give or take." Argus rolled down his sleeves and sat on the sofa. As he did so, Willa caught a glimpse of his ankles. He wasn't wearing any socks, and above his sneakers she could see more eyes. Some were peering up at her, but others were closed.

"They're asleep," explained Argus. "They rest in shifts, so I've always got a few eyes awake and watching."

"Twenty-four-seven!" crooned Tengu with delight. "And his hearing is fantastic too. He can hear a hummingbird spit from three blocks away! Argus can be our watchman. He'll keep track of everything that goes on and report back to you." Tengu gave him a friendly slap on the back, and Argus flinched.

"Did I hit an eye? Sorry, old man," said Tengu.

Argus smiled shyly. His eyes were tired but kind, and even though he was a big man, his movements were slow and gentle. He was getting on in years, not as old as Horace, but still pretty old.

"What's it like?" Willa asked. "Seeing with all those eyes?"

He smiled. "It's not really like seeing. I … absorb my surroundings. It just pours in from all sides." Then he sighed. "It's a little tiring, truth be told."

Willa decided she liked him. "When can you start?"

"I have already," he answered.

"What do you mean?"

Argus took a deep breath. "Since I arrived, a chubby lady tiptoed down the hall into the kitchen, the old gentleman in the last room there has his ear to his door and is listening to our every word," he threw Tengu an uncertain look. "There are odd noises coming from the room Tengu came out of…." Tengu started in surprise, shooting Willa a nervous look.

Argus went on. "I know there are fairies living here, I can tell by the fairy dust on the mantle, but they're staying out of sight. The spider in that bowl up there took a peek and has decided she doesn't like me. Eighteen ants have come out of a hole in the floorboards and are moving along the wall, heading for some muffin crumbs under the sofa. I can hear beetles in your walls too, the clock over the mantle has wound down, a kettle is boiling in the kitchen, and ... you have a pool in the backyard?"

"Yes," answered Willa.

"Someone just fell into it."

Willa raced around the house, with Tengu and Argus close behind. Belle's wheelchair sat empty at the side of the pool, and there were ripples in the dark water.

"BELLE!"

Willa ran up to the edge and stared into the murky depths. Her entire body tensed. She felt an impulse to jump in after her, but it was followed by a wave of nausea and fear. She stood rooted to the ground as Tengu and Argus joined her.

"She's a mermaid, Willa. She'll be okay," said Tengu.

Willa took a breath. "Yes, of course, but... How long can she stay under?"

A white shape appeared in the depths, grew larger, and Belle's head broke the surface, strands of green goo adorning her silver hair. She was grinning.

"Come on in, the water's fine!"

"Omigosh! Belle!" Tengu and Argus were both covering their eyes — quite a challenge for Argus — and backing away. It was only then that Willa noticed Belle's clothes scattered all over the ground.

"Nothing like skinny-dipping!" Belle cackled wickedly.

Tengu dragged Argus away with him. "Come on, let's find you a room to stay in." They broke into a run, escaping into the house.

"Come on in, dearie," said Belle, lazily paddling through the green scum.

"I already told you I can't."

"Just hang on to the side."

Willa flushed. "No! How many times do I have to tell you? I'm not coming in! Ever!"

Belle looked up at her quizzically. Willa took a deep breath. "I'm … scared of the water."

"No, you're not," said Belle.

"I really am! It's a phobia. Weird, I know, but I'm fine with it. It doesn't bother me at all." Willa knew she was babbling, but she couldn't seem to stop. "I don't even want to go in the water. It's too dangerous."

Belle's expression hardened and her eyes narrowed. "Dangerous! Who told you that? Your mother, I bet."

"Sure, I guess. She's got the same phobia."

Belle's face had gone crimson with rage. "Lies! Your mother is filling your head with lies!"

Willa stared at her. "What do you mean?"

Belle's hands slid out of the water and gripped the side of the pool. Her eyes burned into Willa's, but her voice was soft and cold.

"At your house, in the guest room closet, on the top shelf, tucked behind some blankets, is a shoebox. You go home and take a look in that box and then come back and tell me that your mother isn't a liar!" Belle pushed off from the side, turning her back on Willa as she swam away.

Willa's blood ran cold. "Belle!" she called. "What are you talking about? Belle!"

Belle had only one more thing to say before disappearing under the surface again. "Go home, *human!*" she hissed.

Chapter Twelve

A Pandora's box

Willa walked to the front gate. She heard Tengu calling from the porch, but she didn't stop. She didn't want him to see the tears streaming down her face.

Human! She could still hear the anger in Belle's voice.

Hunching forward to keep the rain off her face, she hurried home, her thoughts jumbled. She thought they'd become so close, she thought they were friends. How could things go so wrong so suddenly? Belle had turned on her — why? Because of her stupid water phobia? Her mom never went near the water either; Willa'd never seen her so much as dip her toe into the ocean.

Willa stared at her feet as she strode along, growing more and more angry. *Belle is crazy. How could she say those things about Mom? She doesn't know her. She doesn't know either of us!*

At home, Willa went into the guest room and stared at the closet door. This was the room that Belle stayed in after Eldritch Manor first burned down. It would be just like her to snoop around, so she might actually be right about the shoebox.

"Dinner's in fifteen minutes!" called Mom from downstairs.

"Okay!" replied Willa with a guilty start. She opened the closet door and pulled up a chair to stand on. The upper shelf was filled with blankets and pillows. She took a deep breath and slipped her hand beneath them, reaching all the way to the back. Nothing. She smiled. *Belle was just messing with me. There's nothing here.* Still, she slid her hand along the shelf. She came across the box in the farthest back corner.

It was a cardboard shoebox, and it looked pretty old. It was heavy. Willa stepped down and put the box on the bed. *What on earth could be in there that would be such a big deal?* She really didn't want to open it, but at the same time she was dying to know what was inside. She sat on the bed and lifted the lid.

Newspaper clippings. The top one was about her parents' high school graduation. In the grainy group photo she found Mom and Dad's younger faces. "*Back row, left to right, Maris Godwin, Marvin Fuller...*" Standing next to each other, of course. High-school sweethearts.

Willa flipped through a few more clippings. They all seemed to be from that same era, all about high-school stuff. There were also photos of her parents' friends and family: Grandpa, and Dad with his sister and parents. She found photos of birthday parties, school dances, picnics, old-timey stuff. She lifted the mass of clippings and photos to see what was at the bottom, what was making the box so heavy. Under all the paper was a pile of tarnished medals on faded ribbons. Willa picked one up and turned it over to read the inscription.

"Maris Godwin, Senior Girls' Front Crawl Champion, District Meet 1980."

Willa sat back, stunned. Front crawl? Her mom swam? Not only swam, but swam well? She went through the other medals. They all belonged to her mom. They were all for swimming, and all from the same year, when she was in grade ten. None from grade eleven or twelve. Had she quit?

Willa went back through the stack and found a colour newspaper photo of the swim team. Her mom was front and centre, smiling, full of cheerful confidence, a streak of white hair cutting through the dark locks. *Just like my hair! I've never seen that streak. She's always dying her hair.*

Willa kept rummaging. There were articles about local swim meets, which raved on and on about Maris Godwin. Willa had to shake her head. The idea of her mom being at all athletic was just too weird.

The longest article caught her eye, and she began to read.

"M. Godwin once again dominated the Senior Girls Swim Events with her almost supernatural abilities…"

The word "supernatural" made Willa's blood run cold. She read on.

"Watching her closely as she performed the front crawl, it was this reporter's impression that this young lady doesn't even need to take a breath! She seems to be part fish!"

"Suppertime!" called Mom from downstairs. Willa started guiltily, thrusting everything back into the box.

"Coming! I'm just … washing my hands!" Willa went into the bathroom and shut the door. She turned on the tap and stared at the running water. Belle's words sat cold in her stomach. She was right. Willa looked at herself in the mirror, at the white streak in her own hair. *Mom lied to me. Why?*

At the dinner table, Willa eyed her mom nervously. She couldn't decide how to bring it up. *Maybe I shouldn't. But it's going to drive me crazy if I don't.*

She watched her parents eating and chatting. Dad, with his quiet voice, his hair thinner than in the high school photos, but with the same shy smile. Mom, who now seemed cagey and mysterious, with her hair carefully dyed chestnut brown, and her eyes wary.

They were talking about the weather. The torrential rain had flooded basements all over town, though theirs was still dry — knock on wood. There was a pause in the conversation and Willa dove right in.

"The pool at Eldritch filled up with rainwater," she said.

"That's a crazy amount of rain," marvelled her dad.

"Belle even swam in it."

He chuckled. "Must have been chilly."

Her mom frowned and said nothing.

"She tried to get me to go in, too," continued Willa.

"You told her you don't swim?" her mom asked sharply.

"Yes," Willa said. "I don't swim. And neither do you."

Her mom raised an eyebrow. Dad kept his head down.

"You've never been able to swim, have you?" persisted Willa. "No, wait, I almost forgot … you *did* swim.

In fact, you won a whole bunch of medals for swimming in high school!"

Mom stared, anger flashing in her eyes. "Have you been snooping through my things?"

"I found a box in the guest room." Willa folded her arms. "Did you swim in high school?"

"I don't want to talk about it."

"Did you swim in high school?"

The silence was long and tense. Dad took his plate to the sink and slipped out of the room. *Coward*, thought Willa.

Mom finally answered, her voice hard. "Yes, Willa, I did."

"You told me we both had the same phobia of water. You said you always had it! You lied to me!"

"It's too complicated to get into right now."

"Tell me!"

Her mother frowned, but she seemed to be considering it, so Willa pushed on. "How did you learn to swim? Did Grandpa teach you?"

"No. He said swimming was dangerous. Riptides, undercurrents, that sort of thing." Her mom went to the sink and ran water for the dishes.

"So when did you learn?"

She answered without turning around. "Phys. ed. class in high school. Grandpa wanted to get me excused, but I fought him. He was right, though. I should never have learned to swim."

Willa shook her head. "Why? You were good at it!"

"Yes I was," she answered simply.

Willa lowered her voice, unsure of whether or not she should ask. "Were you good because of Belle? Are you … part mermaid?"

At the sink, her mom stiffened. She whirled to face Willa, her eyes flashing. "Certainly not!"

"But you knew about Belle …"

"I didn't know anything. I thought she was just a regular human. A regular, selfish, heartless, child-abandoning human." Her mom was flushed, breathing heavily.

"When did you find out she was a mermaid?"

Her mom clattered dishes into the sink. "I'd rather not talk about it."

"But I need to know!"

"Don't be so dramatic!" her mom huffed. "I don't *have* to tell you anything!"

Willa pushed on. "Why did you stop swimming?"

"Because water is dangerous."

"Dangerous? That's crazy! There are no riptides in a pool!"

"I think we're done with this conversation." Her mom started for the door. Willa felt panicky — it was now or never. She grabbed her mother's arm.

"We are *not* done! Why did you stop swimming?"

Her mom shook off her hand and drew to her full indignant height. "Willa!"

"WHY DID YOU STOP SWIMMING?" Willa shouted, her heart pounding. Her mom regarded her for a moment, and then her eyes narrowed.

"You really want to know? You really want to know? Well, I'll tell you." She reached out both hands and put them on either side of Willa's head, feeling behind her ears. Willa pulled away.

"What are you doing? Belle did that to me today, the very same thing…."

"Behind your ears. Can you feel two long bumps, like ridges?"

Willa felt with her fingers for a moment. "Yeah, I guess."

"*That's* why I was such a good swimmer, and *that's* why I quit."

Willa waited. Cold fear was collecting in the pit of her stomach. "I don't understand. What are they?"

Her mother looked her in the eye for a moment before answering. "Gills."

Chapter Thirteen

Secrets, lies, and superstition

"WHAT?" Willa backed away, staring at her.

Her mom smoothed her blouse. "Now, if you'll excuse me, I've got some work to do." She turned to leave.

"You can't just tell me that and walk away!" Willa was trembling.

Her mom ran her fingers through her hair, pressing behind her ears in a gesture Willa had seen her do a million times.

"Are they really—?" Willa asked.

"If you don't use them, they close up. I stopped swimming, and they closed up. End of story. Back to normal."

Willa felt the ridges behind her ears again. *Normal.* She felt ill.

"That's why I kept you out of the water," said her mom.

"I stayed out of the water because I was afraid of the water!"

"Right. And that's a good thing."

Willa sank into a chair. Her mom continued.

"I think it would be best if you didn't go to Eldritch Manor any more."

"Why?"

"Belle is not a good influence on you. She's selfish and manipulative, and I don't want you spending any more time with her. From now on I want you to come straight home after school. I'd rather you stayed away from all of them."

"Them? You mean my friends."

"They aren't your only friends. What about the kids at school?"

"I don't have anything in common with them," Willa muttered.

"Well, what on earth do you have in common with those old folks? They do nothing but stir up trouble and put you in danger! They shouldn't even be here! I wish …"

Willa stared at her mom, her eyes filling with tears.

Her mom looked at her sadly. "I wish she'd never come back."

Willa had heard enough. She strode out into the hall and grabbed her coat.

"Willa! Where are you going? It's raining cats and dogs."

"I need to go for a walk…." She stumbled out the door, into the night, and started to run.

Willa ran, blinking away tears, until she found herself in front of Eldritch Manor. She'd taken that route without even thinking. Every window in the house was lit up, but she didn't want to go in. Instead she walked to the backyard.

In the gloom of dusk the pool was a dark, gaping mouth. She stepped up, and her reflection shimmied in the water, staring back. It was her and yet not her. The face couldn't really be seen; the features were lost in darkness, though the moonlight caught the streak of silver in her hair. Every once in a while, a shimmer of bubbles would rise up from the depths, shattering her image across the water's surface.

The silence gave way to a rustling of leaves, growing louder. Willa looked up to see the foliage around her moving — leaves, bushes, grass, the vines on the fence, the branches overhead. She was enveloped in a soft, insistent whisper.

She couldn't stop herself from touching the ridges behind her ears. She was grossed out, though she also felt a stirring of excitement.

Who am I? What am I? Could I really be a mermaid?

Was it possible that the water she had always dreaded was really her home? If it was, why was she so afraid?

She knelt in the wet grass and leaned forward, bringing her face close to the water's surface. She couldn't see more than a few inches into the depths. She closed her eyes and lowered her face into the water. It was cold but soothing. For a moment she felt her mind and body grow calm. Then something brushed her cheek, and she jerked out of the water, falling back into the grass, gasping and trembling.

The water is dangerous. It has to be.

Above her, stars twinkled between the clouds. Willa rose to her feet, took a last look at the pool, and walked away.

Back home, her dad was waiting up for her.

"You okay?" he asked, and Willa nodded. He glanced up the stairs, lowering his voice. "Back in high school, when your mom realized she had …" He pointed to the side of his head. "… you know … well, it was pretty traumatic for her." He smiled. "She does tend to overreact. You know how she is."

"Yeah. Is she still upset?"

"A bit. She just needs to calm down, think things over." He put his arm around her shoulders. "Maybe you both do."

Willa nodded again. "Yeah, I guess so."

Her dad's face brightened. "Would you like the usual for your birthday cake? Angel food with the little coloured bits? And the super fluffy icing? With sprinkles?"

"Sure." Willa gave him a smile. That had been her favourite ever since she was little. This year her birthday had snuck up on her. It just didn't feel as much of a big deal as it used to. "Don't go to any extra trouble, though. Any cake is fine."

"No trouble at all! We'll whip you up a masterpiece. It's not every day our little girl turns into a teenager." He gave her a squeeze. "Goodnight, sweetie."

"Goodnight, Dad."

She fell into bed but slept fitfully, dreaming of deep, black water. She dreamed she was back at the pool. Dead leaves floated on the surface, slowly gathering, rafting together to form a face. There was a breath of a breeze, the eyelids opened to reveal eyes the colour of ash, and Willa pitched forward into the water.

The next morning Willa stayed in her bedroom until her parents had left for work, despite the knocks and calls.

"You'll be late! Get a move on!" called Mom.

"We've got to go. Are you all right in there?" called Dad.

Willa hollered back that she was getting dressed, and listened to them leave. Then she lay in bed for another few blessed minutes, even though she knew it would make her incredibly late for school.

Does she really mean it? she wondered glumly. *Do I have to come straight home after school? Am I really grounded?*

At school she shunned everyone even more than usual. She felt their eyes on her and kept putting her hand to her head, patting her hair down over the … ridges.

Can anyone see them?

In the library, she looked so glum that the guidance counsellor, Miss Grimes, sat across from her.

"Is anything wrong, Willa?" she asked gently.

Willa shook her head.

"Everything all right at home?"

"Yes."

"Nothing you want to talk about?"

Willa looked into her kindly blue eyes, summoned up a smile, and shook her head. *If you only knew!*

Outside the school, she paused for a moment, then turned toward Eldritch Manor. Of course. Her parents wouldn't be home for another forty-five minutes at least, so she could fit in a quick visit. The thought of being cooped up at home against her will made her furious. As she trudged along, she noticed it was brighter. The clouds were thinning, and the rain had lessened to a light drizzle.

She wanted to curl up on the sofa in the parlour and think, but when she opened the front door she was surrounded by a crowd of eager faces. Everyone but Belle, she noticed.

"Is your birthday really tomorrow?" asked Tengu. "Argus told us." Behind him, Argus blushed and looked at the floor.

"How old will you be? Twenty-six ... twenty-seven?" asked Robert.

Baz elbowed him. "She's turning eighteen, you ninny."

Willa smiled. "Thirteen, actually."

"Thirteen?" gasped Baz, putting her hands to her head in horror. "And Walpurgis Night still a whole month away!"

"Okay, what is Walpurgis Night?" asked Willa, but Baz was walking in circles around her and making strange gestures with her hands. "What are you doing?" Willa looked to the others. "What is she doing?"

"Baz is a little superstitious," explained Horace, though he, too, was looking at Willa strangely. In fact, they were all staring at her.

"Your birthday is April Fools' Day! You're going to be *thirteen* on April Fools' Day!" Tengu suddenly exclaimed.

"Thirteen!" wailed Baz, reversing her direction and pacing backward around Willa.

"Oh, for heaven's sake," said Willa. "It's just a number."

"Thirteen can sometimes be lucky," suggested Fjalarr.

"She's turning into a teenager," observed Robert.

Fjalarr made a face. "Ooh. Not lucky. Poor kid."

"Thirteen *can* be a symbol of momentous change," admitted Horace.

"See, that's good, right?" asked Willa hopefully.

"Momentous change, revolution, upheaval, ruin, apocalypse ..." intoned Horace.

"Teenage boys," added Robert, and they all shook their heads.

"All right already! Enough!" exclaimed Willa hotly. "Let's just forget about my birthday!" They moved away, still eyeing her and whispering. Argus was the only one who lingered. He coughed apologetically.

"Would you like a report?"

"What? Oh, yeah, I suppose so."

Argus cleared his throat and recited dutifully. "Eldritch Manor surveillance report, March thirty-first. The fairies were partying late last night. They kept everyone awake with their singing, and now most of the dwarves are napping. Baz has eaten so many beetles that she has a stomache ache. Tabitha's stitches seem to be getting even smaller, and it's really affecting our time. By my calculation, each hour of real world time lasts about three hours in here. Tengu *still* has something you don't know about concealed in his room, and —"

"What has he got?" Willa interrupted.

"I promised him I wouldn't tell," said Argus. "I'm sorry, but he did save my life once, so I owe him."

"All right, I'll check it out. What else?"

"The lady in that room there…" He pointed.

"Miss Trang."

"I hear her snoring; she's been asleep ever since I arrived. Is that normal?"

"Yes. She's a dragon. She hibernated all winter. Anything else?"

"Belle went for a midnight swim. She returned to her room at 1:22 a.m. and hasn't come out or spoken to anyone since. Not even to complain about the fairies, which is rather … out of character."

Willa nodded. "Is she in there now?"

"Yes."

"Her mood?" asked Willa.

"Surly. With a touch of indignation."

Just then Willa's eye was caught by a small motion. She looked down and saw Tabitha scurry into the parlour.

"Okay, thanks Argus," said Willa. He nodded and headed for the kitchen.

Willa stared at Belle's door for a moment and then turned away. She didn't want to see her, not right now. Belle would just rant about her mom, and at the moment Willa wanted a break from both of them.

She thought about finding out what Tengu was hiding in his room, but decided she didn't really care. Then she considered talking to Tabitha again about the size of her stitches, but she knew the spider was doing her best. Instead, she climbed the stairs to the unfinished second storey, stepping out of a trapdoor into the fresh air. Above her head, the attic bobbed gently in the breeze. She grabbed the rope, pulled it down, and climbed inside.

Roshni sat on her perch, eyeing her in a friendly way. Willa ran a hand over the bird's feathers. Her eyes strayed to the windows. To her great surprise, she could see the town below quite clearly.

The cloud the dwarves made, it must be like one-way glass! Nice. Gazing down at the streets and houses, Willa wondered how human she really was, and suddenly felt very alone. The room swayed gently. It was like being on a boat. All she could hear were leaves rustling and tree branches creaking in the wind.

Willa looked out the windows, one by one, first toward Hanlan's Hill, then out to the distant sea, then in the direction of home and school, then finally she turned and looked down at their own yard. The pool looked very different from so far above. It sparkled like a black jewel, and Willa stared at it, transfixed.

Chapter Fourteen

In which Willa turns lucky thirteen

Willa stood looking down into the pool, but instead of water it was filled with lush, green leaves. She leaned forward and dived in, swimming down through endless green. Then a space opened before her, and the leaves began to form a face: grey, wideset eyes under straight, level brows, a long, thin nose, and a serious mouth. Willa swam and swam but came no closer. She sent out a thought:

Who are you?

After a moment the lips parted, and—

"Wake up! It's nine o'clock! You're late for school!"

Willa started, tumbling out of bed.

"What? I just—" She grabbed her clock. It was 7:27. Dad stood laughing in the doorway.

"You stinker!" She flung her pillow at him.

"Gotcha! And it's Saturday, too! Happy April Fools' birthday!" He disappeared.

She sat down on the bed and sighed.

April Fool, that's me. A freak with gills. And lucky thirteen, too. Whoop-de-doo.

Her slippers were filled with shaving cream, there was mayonnaise in her tube of toothpaste, and the bathroom tap sprayed right in her face when she turned it on. Her dad, usually a pretty boring guy, absolutely *lived* for pranks.

She could hear her parents in the kitchen as she tip-toed toward the front door. She wasn't in the mood for acting cheerful in front of her mom. She felt strangely drawn to go look in the pool.

"Where are you going, birthday girl?"

It was her dad. Willa thought quick, answering in a whisper. "I'm meeting some kids from school. We're pranking one of the teachers." She hated to lie to her dad, but she knew this would get him onside right away.

He grinned. "Nothing causing property damage or physical harm, I hope."

"Nope."

"Off you go then. I'll cover for you, but don't be long." He gave her a wink and disappeared into the kitchen. Willa left feeling absolutely wretched.

The sun was peeking through the clouds and burst through in full force as she came through the Eldritch front gate. She lifted her face to the warm rays. *Sunshine at last!*

She started back toward the pool but heard someone calling her name. Mrs. Norton was hurrying out the front door and down the walk.

"Willa! Hello! I've got a little emergency on my hands … I just left Everett with your friend, Miss…" she made vague forgetful hand motions. "Oh, I've forgotten her name. I think it started with an M — tall young lady, with long blonde hair?"

"Young lady?" Willa frowned, but Mrs. Norton continued in a breathless rush.

"Anyway, Everett was sound asleep, and she said you'd be here any minute and then I saw you coming down the street, so I put him in the parlour ... Can't stay another second ... We've got a flooded basement and the twins with the flu! I'll be back for him once we're done bailing ourselves out! Thank youuuu!" And with a wave she was gone.

Willa watched her go, then opened the front door and ran straight into the chandelier. She stared at it. The crystals were the wrong way around. The chandelier was now attached to the floor at her feet and standing upright, with the crystals dangling upward somehow.

Laughter sounded from above, and Willa lifted her eyes to see a crowd of dwarves on the ceiling, cheerfully defying gravity.

"April Fool!" crowed Fjalarr.

"How are you doing that?" stammered Willa, drawing more laughter. Then she noticed several coats hanging upward from hooks on the wall.

I'm the one who's on the ceiling!

In a panic, she threw her arms around the chandelier, just as she felt the pull of gravity reverse. The next thing she knew, she was hanging upside down and shrieking for help.

The hall carpet was yanked out from the feet of the dwarves and flew up to her, guided by a dozen giggling fairies.

"Hop on," chortled Sarah. Just then the chandelier ripped free of the ceiling. Willa screamed, but the fairies caught her and the chandelier in the carpet and lowered them gently to the floor.

Willa looked up in time to see the front door she had just walked through slowly slide down the wall until it was back where it should be. The dwarves bowed to Willa, and before she could say what was on her mind, Fjalarr stepped forward and handed her a wrapped present.

"Happy birthday from all of us!"

Willa took a deep breath, and her good humour returned. "Thank you. That was quite … something."

"Willa, come in here and sit down!" Tengu appeared, grabbing her arm and pulling her into the parlour. He pointed to an armchair. "Sit here!"

Willa looked around the parlour. Robert, Horace, and Baz were there, and the dwarves trooped in as well. But no Belle. And no baby carriage.

"Where's Everett?"

Baz looked at her blankly. "Who's Everett?"

"The baby! Mrs. Norton said she left him in the parlour. With a young lady, which doesn't make sense...."

Baz shrugged. Tengu tugged on Willa's sleeve. "Sit here, Willa!"

"No, hold on, I've got to find—" A box of chocolates was thrust into her face, flown in by more laughing fairies.

"Um, thank you," sighed Willa. She gingerly pulled off the lid and was rewarded with a dazzling spray of rainbow-coloured sparks. Startled, Willa dropped the box and fell backward over a rabbit kneeling on the floor behind her. She landed heavily in the chair, from which sounded a loud raspberry. Tengu was laughing so hard that tears rolled down his cheeks.

"Whoopee cushion!" he gasped. "I love whoopee cushions!"

"Very funny," said Willa. "Now where is baby Everett? Anyone?"

Silence fell over the room. Willa felt alarm take hold of her. "Mrs. Norton said she left Everett with a 'tall young woman with long blonde hair.'"

No response, just a lot of blank looks. Willa struggled to keep calm.

"Listen. No more April Fools' stuff. I'm serious. Who has Everett? The only person I can think of with long blonde hair is Mab, but she…" Willa stopped in her tracks. "Mab?" She started for the wasp nest.

"She's not there," said Sarah.

"Sarah! Is Mab behind this? Where is she?" Sarah pursed her lips, not answering. "And where's Oberon? Why is it sunny again? Have they stopped fighting?" Willa spun around to Argus, just entering the parlour. "Argus! What's going on?"

Argus cleared his throat and began calmly. "Eldritch Manor surveillance report, April first. Various pranks have been in play since daybreak, a few of which you have encountered. The refrigerator has stopped working. Tengu *still* has something in his room you don't know about."

Horace jumped to his feet and glared at Tengu. "I thought so!" he exclaimed, striding from the room. Tengu followed him, protesting.

"Horace, wait! I can explain!"

Bewildered, Willa watched them leave, then grabbed Argus's arm. "Where's the baby?"

Argus hung his head. "Oberon came to me with a startling report about some kind of evil presence in the woods and asked me to come with him to check it out. When I got out there I was overcome by a sleep spell."

Willa began to pace. "So Oberon got you out of the house and put you to sleep, then Mab ... can she change her form?"

Everyone nodded.

"So she changed to human size and took the baby." Willa paused. "But why would she go to all that trouble?"

"It *is* odd," admitted Argus slowly. "I haven't heard of fairies stealing human babies for at least a hundred years."

"Stealing babies?" gasped Willa. "What are you talking about?"

"It's something fairies do," said Baz simply. "Everyone knows that."

"It's something they *did*," corrected Argus.

"What did they do with them?"

"With what?" asked Baz.

"The babies! What did they do with them?" Willa was on the edge of total panic.

"Took them for their own. Fed them fairy food, that kind of thing."

"Why feed them fairy food?"

Baz responded slowly, as if speaking to someone with no brains. "Any human who eats fairy food must dwell in the land of fairies forever. How can you not know that?"

Willa turned again to Sarah. "Where is she? Where's Mab?"

Sarah's eyes were wide with alarm, but her lips remained pursed shut.

"Tell me, Sarah, please!" pleaded Willa.

"She can't talk about it. She's under a spell," murmured Argus. "Shall we search the house?"

"Yes, yes! You take this floor. Look in every room! I'll go upstairs! Robert, take the basement, and dwarves, search the woods! Go, go!" Willa ran into the hall. She could hear Horace and Tengu arguing in Tengu's room as she raced past and up the stairs. From the second floor she heard Robert thundering down the ramp and the dwarves piling out the front door. She clambered up into the floating attic room.

"Roshni! I need your help! Can you fly around and look for baby Everett? Mab's taken him somewhere. Hurry!"

Roshni gave a quick nod, hopped out the open door, and swooped high into the sky. Willa took advantage of the view, wildly scanning the backyard and the woods.

Then she heard loud voices, and Horace appeared around the corner of the house with Tengu running along behind. Horace was holding a small object wrapped in a blanket.

"Everett!" breathed Willa. "Thank goodness." Tengu was shouting at Horace. She strained to hear him.

"I can take good care of him! He's like my own child! Please!"

Willa frowned. *Tengu took Everett? That makes no sense.*

Horace turned angrily on Tengu, but Willa couldn't hear his response. Then he strode on toward the pool.

Willa dropped out of the attic and threw herself down the stairs and out the front door, pushing aside a very surprised Argus. She rounded the house just in time to see Horace holding the small form above the pool.

"Horace, no!" hollered Willa. Surprised, Horace turned to look at her as he dropped the bundle into the water.

Willa shrieked. Propelled by a force too strong to resist, she ran and felt a strange thrill of freedom as she threw herself headlong into the dark water of the pool.

Chapter Fifteen

Full Fathom Five

Darkness all around. Willa kept her eye on the white spot below her, sinking into the depths.

She chased it, flailing with her arms and kicking wildly. She tried not to think about the cold and the whooshing around her ears, the tendrils tickling her arms and legs, the dark shadows darting through the gloom. She knew she couldn't think about anything but that bundle in front of her.

As she reached out for it, she had the sudden thought, *something isn't right*, as the cloth fell away and a glistening black shape darted out of it.

Willa had only time for a glimpse of a weird bird-like head, bound with a cloth blindfold. With a strong whip of its snake-body, the creature zigzagged rapidly toward the surface.

What the heck was that?

Willa watched it disappear into the glare of daylight so distant above her. She became aware of the pressure of the water; a chill shot through her, and she wavered dizzily.

Then the terror hit. Her limbs felt encased in ice. The reality of having no air in her lungs hit her too. The pressure in her throat and head was agonizing. Her lungs throbbed and gaped inside her; she was a deflated balloon folding in on herself. White spots swam before her eyes, and then a dark curtain fell across her sight.

Her drift into unconsciousness was interrupted by a violent tearing, a burning, ripping sensation in her head. Her mouth opened to scream, but the pain suddenly fell away and oxygen flowed into her lungs. She gasped, and her vision cleared. All at once she could see her surroundings with astonishing clarity. No longer murky, the water was now filled with colour and movement. Gulping in delicious breaths of air, she looked around in wonder.

Willa was floating in a deep turquoise night filled with stars. Masses of golden and green ribbons rose from below, stretching upward in a gently waving forest. The fluorescent glimmer of a hundred tiny fish undulated before her, reminding Willa that she was underwater. She was underwater and she was breathing.

Her hands shot up, and she felt behind her ears. Two long folds in her skin opened and shut in rhythm with the rise and fall of her chest. She shut her mouth and plugged her nose, but found she was still inhaling and exhaling.

Gills! she thought. *Gills.*

But was it really so awful? It didn't seem so bad right now. She was alive. She was underwater and could stay under as long as she liked. And she wasn't afraid. That irrational terror, the phobia that had dogged every day of her life, had evaporated in the first rush of air through her gills.

Darkling Green

I am not afraid of the water.
Water is not dangerous.

The extent of her mother's deception astonished her. *How could she keep all this from me? And why? This is ...* She couldn't find words for it. The easy floating feeling, the drifting, the cool, the calm. It was the most peaceful sensation she'd ever felt. It felt ... right. It just felt right. She kicked, glided, rolled, and flipped. It was glorious, this feeling. It was like flying.

She cruised along for a while, inspecting the sea life, the brilliant patches of coral and the fish of infinite variety and hue.

How could all this be in our pool? she wondered briefly. Gazing down, she caught sight of the time holes: two silver bubbles below her, nestled in the rocks and coral. The idea of a gateway to another time filled her with a giddy desire to plunge into them. Her mind was light and easy. It was as if all gravity had been sucked out of the world, and she laughed suddenly, sending up sparkling clouds of bubbles.

Looking up, Willa saw the light above her, and it all rushed back into her mind. Up there, somewhere, was Everett. She had to find him and make sure he was all right.

She rose up, and the patch of daylight grew larger. When she could make out figures and faces peering down into the water, she paused.

I don't want to go up. I want to stay down here.

She suddenly understood Belle's obsession with the pool. It was definitely not the pit of muddy water and slime it had seemed before. This was a whole new world.

With a bubbly sigh, she gave a last kick, and her head burst into the sunshine. She was momentarily blinded but heard gasps from all sides.

"Willa! Are you all right?"

"Thank heavens!"

"I told you she was fine!" crowed Belle, leaning forward in her chair.

"You've been down there for ages!"

"Seventeen minutes," offered Argus.

"Seventeen? Psh! She could stay down there all day if she wanted to!" cackled Belle.

Willa felt the sides of her head again, felt the bumps behind her ears. A hand was offered, and she grabbed it. Argus lifted her out of the water and gently set her on the grass. Someone draped a towel around her. It was warm in the sunshine.

"What was that black thing in the water?" Willa asked.

Tengu stepped forward with the shiny, horrible wriggly creature. The head looked like a chicken, but it wasn't fluffy; it was smooth and black. A strip of cloth covered its eyes. The body was vaguely chicken-like, tapering into a long black snake tail.

"It's a basilisk!" announced Tengu proudly.

"Don't they turn you to stone just by looking at you?" yelped Willa.

"That's why I put the blindfold on."

Horace looked at him sternly. "That is what Tengu has been hiding in his room, ever since it dropped out of one of the time holes."

"He was just a baby when he fell out of that hole, a

poor little orphan. His eyes hadn't even opened yet."

Willa looked up at Horace. "Why did you throw him in the pool?"

"We shouldn't be messing with such a dangerous creature. I thought he'd go back through the time hole."

Tengu grinned at her. "Thank you for jumping in after him, Willa, but you needn't have worried. Basilisks are very good swimmers."

"I, um … I didn't really…." started Willa nervously. *I jumped in because I thought Horace was trying to drown baby Everett.* She sighed. No need to go there. "You're welcome." She looked around the group. "Has anyone found Everett?"

She heard a screech as a shadow passed overhead. Willa looked up, shielding her eyes. "Roshni! Have you seen him? Where is he?"

Roshni answered with a squawk and swooped up to land in a nearby treetop.

"Way up there? Good grief. Someone get me a ladder!"

Argus found one in the stable and held it against the tree while Willa climbed to the top. Poking her head up through the leaves, she found Everett snoozing in a hammock of vines under a leafy umbrella held by Oberon. Mab was there, too, trying to shoo Roshni away.

"Shush! Get lost! Scram!"

"Mab!"

Mab froze for a moment, then turned sheepishly to face her. "Willa! Hello!"

"You stole baby Everett!"

"Baby Evvie-wevvie needed fresh air and sunshine."

Out of the corner of her eye Willa saw Oberon slip something behind his back. "What's that? What are you hiding?"

He reluctantly pulled out a tiny plate of berries.

"Is that fairy food? Did you feed him fairy food?" Willa demanded.

Oberon frowned. "We didn't get a chance! He's been asleep the whole time!"

Just then Everett opened his eyes, looked around, and let out a happy gurgle. Oberon groaned. "*Now* he wakes up!"

Willa gently lifted Everett and pressed him to her as she carefully descended the ladder. Argus rescued the baby carriage from a nearby bush, and Willa tucked Everett into it before turning back to Mab.

"You *cannot* steal babies, Mab! What were you thinking?"

Mab pouted. "We used to do it all the time."

"I don't care!" Willa shook her finger at both fairies. "You must never, EVER come near Everett again. Or any other human baby! EVER! Do you hear me?"

"I told her it was a bad idea," said Oberon.

"What?" Mab turned on him. "The whole thing was *your* idea! You said stealing human babies reminded you of the good old days!"

"All I said was, 'Wouldn't it be fun to steal a baby'... I didn't really mean it."

"Liar!"

"Kidnapper!"

"Troll!"

"Harpy!"

As the two fairies glowered at each other, clouds crowded in front of the sun.

"And there goes the sunshine," Willa observed with a shiver. The crowd around the pool dispersed into the house. Mab and Oberon flew off, glaring daggers at each other. Only Argus remained behind.

"This is all my fault, Willa. I will pack my things and go."

"Argus, no! I really need your help. Please, please stay," begged Willa, picking one of his eyes to look at. "Please?"

Argus blushed. "All right. But from now on, when Everett is in the house I will not leave his side. And I will no longer believe anything the fairies tell me." He held out his hand, and Willa shook it.

"Don't worry about Everett. I'm going to tell Mrs. Norton I don't have time to babysit anymore. Not trusting the fairies, though, *that's* a good idea."

As they pushed the carriage toward the house, Willa gave him a sly smile.

"Pack your things? You didn't bring any 'things.'"

Argus pulled a toothbrush from his pocket. "I didn't say it would take long."

Tengu's bedroom door was ajar. Willa peeked in to see Tengu and Horace watching the baby basilisk, still blindfolded, batting a ball of string between its long black tail and its chicken feet. Horace was shaking his head.

"I don't know, Tengu. It's absolutely unprecedented."

Willa joined them. "What is?"

"Keeping a basilisk as a pet! Unprecedented and insane."

At Horace's words, the basilisk hissed at them, revealing a long black snake tongue within its beak. Then he began sharpening his talons on Tengu's dresser, leaving deep scratches in the wood.

Willa turned back to Tengu. "What about this 'turning to stone' business? Are you going to keep him blindfolded forever?"

Tengu whistled between his teeth. The basilisk hopped up onto his arm and rested his head on Tengu's shoulder, making an odd gurgling sound.

"Hear that? He's purring!" said Tengu proudly. "He would never turn me to stone." At Horace and Willa's doubtful looks he added, "I don't think."

"Tengu—" started Horace.

"I'm working with him and training him, and I think I can teach him to not turn us to stone. I'm pretty sure I can, but I would love to have your help, Horace."

Horace looked at him in surprise. "Me?" He scratched his head and stared at the basilisk. "It would be an interesting experiment, I suppose…." His voice trailed off in the way it did when he was immersed in a problem. Willa smiled and turned to go. Tengu gave her an excited thumbs-up as she shut the door behind her.

She turned to find Belle parked there, looking very smug. They looked at each other for a long, long time. Belle reached her hands up to Willa's ears, but Willa pushed them away.

"Yes, they're there," she said crossly.

Belle sat back with a satisfied grin. She patted the sides of her own head. "Just … like … me."

Darkling Green

"I'm going home," said Willa. "I've had enough weirdness for one day."

When Willa returned home, her parents were still in the kitchen preparing her birthday breakfast. Time at Eldritch had slowed so much that she'd only been gone for about twenty minutes.

Willa ducked into the bathroom and took a quick shower to get the last of the algae out of her hair. Then she stared at herself in the mirror. Her hair positively shone, the silver streak even brighter than before.

Is swimming good for my hair, or is it just the algae?

She turned her head from side to side, making sure her hair totally covered the gills. If her mom saw them ... Willa smiled. The swimming business would be her own little secret, for now at least.

At dinnertime, Grandpa arrived for a little birthday celebration.

"Willa the Wisp!" he called from the front door, and Willa ran to give him a big hug. Tonight Grandpa was his usual boisterous self, brimming over with jokes and stories, and Dad tried his best to keep the mood light, but Mom remained distant and wouldn't meet Willa's eye. Willa wasn't exactly in a party mood, either; she was so exhausted, she could barely keep up with conversation.

After dinner, Grandpa sat on the sofa beside her, and she laid her head on his shoulder.

"You seem pretty tired, kiddo. Homework keeping you up at night?"

"No, not really. I just had a long day." She looked into his kind eyes and felt a sudden urge to unburden herself and tell him that she knew about Mom's swimming, that she had jumped in a pool today and could breath underwater! It was all so new and exciting that she desperately wanted to share it with him.

Her mother, however, was watching from across the room, and Willa was just too tired to go through any more drama today. It was all she could do to stay awake for the usual birthday rituals: the cake, the singing, the candles, and her presents — a new sweater and a couple of books. After Grandpa left she announced that she was going to bed.

"Goodnight, birthday girl," said her dad, giving her a hug.

"Bed at eight thirty? Do you feel all right?" asked her mom.

"I'm just tired."

Her mom hugged her, then looked her in the eyes. "Happy birthday, hon. I love you."

Willa nodded and went to her room. She was asleep before her head hit the pillow.

She was swimming again, and ahead of her was the leafy face. The great, grey eyes bordered with leaves watched her quietly. She sent him her question once more.

Who are you?

The whole world fell silent. Willa waited. The mouth opened slowly, revealing an inky black void. Then there was movement within the darkness, and snakey masses of vines burst from the mouth, pouring out with a roar and a crash.

Willa started awake. Her room swam into focus. The clock said 2:00 a.m.

April Fool! she thought.

Chapter Sixteen

A dolphin leads the way

The day after Willa's birthday, she walked to Eldritch Manor with only one thought in her mind: *I want to swim again.*

She intended to go straight to the pool and dive in, but Argus was sitting on the front porch, so she joined him.

"Eldritch Manor surveillance report, April second. Mab and Oberon are sulking about the baby fiasco and blaming each other, hence the cloudy weather. Baz is in the parlour staring at Tabitha, which is making everyone nervous. Horace and Tengu spend all their time locked up with that *thing*...." Argus didn't think much of the basilisk. "The dwarves are working on the second floor rooms and getting a lot done because of the long days, which by my calculation are now approximately eighty-two hours long. All those extra hours are tiring everyone out. We're setting some world records for napping around here."

Willa thanked him and hurried to the backyard. Even though the pool was still murky and streaked with algae, to her the water now appeared soft, shimmery, and inviting. She couldn't even remember how she'd thought it looked gross. Trembling, Willa stripped down to a T-shirt and gym shorts and dove in.

She had a moment of panic when she tried to inhale and couldn't, but then she felt her gills pull open, and she breathed easily. She looked around at the coral and plants and fish that were invisible when she was out of the water. The time bubbles lay far below her, and she decided to keep her distance. She wasn't sure if things might still pop out of them. What if another basilisk tumbled out? Or something worse? No, today she just wanted to enjoy being in the water; the grace and ease of motion was exhilarating. After an hour of drifting, spinning, swooping, and dancing, she grabbed on to a vine growing up the side of the pool and climbed out.

Standing there in the grass, she felt heavy, shackled once more by gravity. Her limbs were awkward and unwieldy. Her mind, too, felt leaden and slow under a blanket of dark clouds. She dried herself off, slowly becoming aware of a figure in the window watching her: Belle.

She turned away and pulled dry clothes on over the wet. She slapped a ballcap over her wet hair, stuffed her towel into her backpack, and strode out of the yard.

It turned out that Tabitha's extra-fine stitchery and the resulting extension of time helped Willa conceal her visits from her mom. If she hurried over right after school, she could stay for a couple of hours, then come home, where barely any time had passed.

So Willa visited Eldritch Manor every day, first stepping inside to say hello, checking in with Argus, maybe tidying up a bit, and then going out to the pool for a dip. After that, a quick hair-rinse in the sink to remove the algae, and she was on her way home. Her mom sometimes commented on how slowly she walked home from school.

"I was hanging out with my friends," she'd answer, which was technically true and pleased her mom, but she still felt guilty about lying. *I'm mad at my mom for lying to me, so I'm lying to her in return,* she thought sadly. She wanted to tell her the truth, and every day she resolved to do it, then lost her nerve. She knew her mom would freak out, and right now she couldn't bear to give up her visits to Eldritch and her daily swim. So the days went on, and the deceit continued.

Willa swam a little longer each day and began diving deeper. The size and depth of the pool varied from day to day. Some days it retained its rectangular shape and felt more like a pool, but on other days the sides receded, revealing caves and tunnels. Some were bright with rainbow coral and neon fish, while others were darker, home to jewelled seahorses and lurking octopi. Since she didn't have to return to the surface for air, she became totally immersed in her exploration and lost all track of time. The longer she swam, the stronger she felt, and the more relaxed she was when she returned to the world above.

Green and more green surrounded her. Willa swam through the leaves until she came face to face with him again. She looked into the grey eyes, eyes empty of meaning, and once again she asked—

Who are you?

—hoping for a different result, but once again the mouth opened and foliage came crashing out, a fury of thorns and branches that swept Willa backward. She tumbled over and over as vines snaked around and past her, carrying her along in their current. Then, as suddenly as it had begun, the greenery calmed, and Willa was lying in a forest.

All was still, but Willa felt she was being watched. She looked up to see brilliant violet eyes peering back at her from the darkness. These eyes weren't like the grey ones. These eyes were full of kindness and concern, and Willa was comforted.

The dream faded peacefully, and Willa slept on. In the morning she woke with the image of those violet eyes imprinted on her mind.

One day Willa was floating above the time holes, thinking about the weird dreams she'd been having, when a dolphin slipped out of the larger bubble. He slid past her, slowing just enough for her to rub his side and take hold of his dorsal fin. The dolphin took her for a thrilling ride, bucking and banking around the rectangle of the pool at top speed. Then, accelerating out of a loop-de-loop, he zoomed down toward the time holes. A silvery blob loomed before them, and before Willa knew what was happening, they had slipped into it.

It was dark. Willa let go of the dolphin, who swam off without her. When her eyes got used to the gloom, she saw she was in a tunnel with proper walls, floor, and ceiling. It was wide enough that she couldn't touch both sides at once. The dolphin was now just a slip of grey disappearing into the distance. She reassured herself that the bubble was close at hand; from this side it looked like a disc of smoked glass with daylight filtering through. Willa touched it and her hand easily passed through it. Then she poked her head through, just to make sure her own pool was still on the other side. Drawing back into the darkness of the time hole, Willa could just make out a light at the far end of the tunnel. Her heart thumped in her chest. She hesitated, caught between fear and curiosity, until the distant chittering of the dolphin persuaded her to take a quick look.

Willa swam cautiously toward the light, which turned out to be another disc just like the first. She could hear seagulls. Taking a deep breath, Willa pushed her head and shoulders through to the other side.

Sunshine beat down on her face. Her eyes adjusted, and she gazed out at a sparkling lagoon, complete with an arc of white sandy beach and a lush jungle beyond. She saw her friend the dolphin leaping in the air and splashing down again. She took a deep breath of fragrant summertime air and gazed around once more before withdrawing and swimming back through the tunnel.

Slipping through the disc at the other end, she breathed a little easier to be back in her own pool. As she emerged from the water, she found Belle waiting patiently for her. They hadn't spoken since her first dip in the pool on her birthday, though Belle was obviously quite pleased about it all.

"You don't need to be swimming in your undies, you know."

Willa clambered out and sat on the edge. "They're gym shorts, not underwear. And you may like skinny-dipping, but I'm not doing it!"

"Oh, heavens to Betsy, who said anything about skinny-dipping?" Belle grumbled. She had something in her lap, which she offered to Willa. It was a bathing suit, green and blue, with silver piping around the edges. Willa gave Belle a big grin.

"Thanks, Belle. I love it."

"You should come and get me when you go for a swim," Belle chided her. "I've got so much to teach you."

Willa felt a sudden urge to share her adventures. "I went into a time hole! A dolphin came through it, and I followed him back to a beach and a jungle."

Belle looked at her in alarm. "Did you leave the tunnel?"

"No, I wasn't sure if that was safe."

"Good instinct. You are perfectly safe as long as you stay inside the tunnel. Going out at the other end is risky."

"Why?"

"Time holes are always moving around."

Willa pointed at the pool. "These ones aren't."

"Yes, for some reason they seem pretty stable at this end. Even Horace isn't sure why. At the other end, how-ever, that's another story. If you leave the tunnel there, you might turn around and find it's disappeared on you, and there's no way back again."

"So if I went through that same one again…?"

"You'll come out somewhere completely different every time."

"Wow." Willa stared down at the silver blobs. Now she could see why Belle had been so intrigued by them.

"We could take another look right now," suggested Belle.

"No, I've got to get home," said Willa quickly. She still hadn't told Belle about her mom banning her from visiting. "But how about tomorrow?"

Belle grinned and nodded. "It's a date."

Chapter Seventeen

Floods, Foliage, and Time Travel

The next day was Saturday, and it suddenly dawned on Willa that it wouldn't be easy to sneak over to Eldritch without school as a cover.

"I'm going for a walk," she announced after breakfast.

"Not in the pouring rain you aren't. I heard you coughing earlier," her mom countered. "It's a perfect day for curling up with a good book."

So Willa curled up with a good book … and stared at the same page for what seemed like two hours but was really fifteen minutes. She stared at the clock in disbelief. *Is Tabitha affecting time here too?*

Then she sat wondering where the time holes might lead, and what it would be like to go for a swim with Belle. She wondered how Tengu and Horace were getting along with the basilisk, and if Oberon and Mab were still fighting.

Looming above these thoughts, however, was the image of cool, rippling water. Willa was positively itching to get into the pool for a swim. She paced around her room, stared out at the rain, and then paced some more.

She took a really long bath. *Just like Belle always does*, she thought, finally understanding why. Even in a small tub, the water sloshing around her was soothing. It filled her ears, beautifully muting the outside world.

And to think I used to hate getting water in my ears!

Somehow she got through the weekend and Monday at school. When she arrived at Eldritch Manor, however, she opened the front door to total chaos. The ramp to the basement was open, lined with dwarves handing up buckets full of water. Argus emerged from the kitchen with an armful of empty buckets.

"Argus, what's going on?"

He stood at attention. "Eldritch Manor surveillance report, April twelfth. The basement is flooded. We're bailing Robert out." And he handed Willa a bucket.

So much for swimming, thought Willa, and got to work. The water in the basement was up to her knees. She scooped up a bucketful and handed it up the line. At the top of the ramp, Argus and Eikinskjaldi were running full buckets into the kitchen, dumping them out and bringing back the empties. They slogged away for hours, until Willa's shoulders and back ached, but without much effect on the level of the water.

When Willa returned the next day, everyone had given up on the basement and Robert had moved into the crowded parlour. Tempers were fraying already. Robert complained about the rabbits underfoot, and Oberon resented having to share the room with someone that immense.

"He's like a walking barnyard," sniffed the fairy king.

Willa ducked out during the squabble that followed

and knocked on Belle's door. "Meet you at the pool!" called Belle. "I'll just be a minute!"

It was quiet in the backyard. Tengu was walking the basilisk around on a little leash.

"Hi, Willa! We're just out for a bit of fresh air!" he called cheerfully as the blindfolded beast walked straight into a tree.

Baz was on her hands and knees in the bushes nearby, pouncing on bugs and popping them into her mouth. Willa shuddered. Even though she knew Baz was just acting out her cat nature, it was still alarming to see an old lady crawling around eating insects.

"All those bugs can't be good for you," she called, but Baz ignored her. Willa breathed in the damp air and gazed around the yard. She was surrounded by new growth. Green shoots were popping up all over, tree trunks were fuzzy with moss, and the stable roof was covered with a green shag carpet.

Willa's eyes were caught by one ropey vine, larger and darker than the rest, that emerged from the pool and disappeared in the mud and wet leaves. She walked over and kicked at it. It was heavy and very solid. Willa leaned down to brush off the leaves and began to follow it into the trees. Tengu joined her, the basilisk in his arms.

"Check out this vine, Tengu. I want to see where it goes."

They followed it through the forest, brushing aside smaller vines and curling tendrils. The only sound was the squelching of their boots in the mud. Willa suddenly felt fearful. Just when the going got very difficult, the trees ended and they found themselves at the stone wall that ran along the back of the property. The vine ended in a mass of green growing up the wall, obscuring half of it.

Tengu let out a low whistle. "That's new," he said.

"New? What do you mean?"

"I could see the whole wall yesterday. That grew in overnight."

"Impossible." Willa stared at the growth. There was a central, thicker mass of leaves at the base of the wall.

A loud crunch made them jump. Baz had walked up behind them, chewing on a large beetle. Its waving legs hung out of her mouth.

"Ew." Willa winced. Baz crunched the bug again and swallowed it down, grinning. Tengu took the basilisk indoors for some warm milk, while Willa paused to peer into the pool.

"The big vine is the one that's growing out of the time hole! It has its roots in another time altogether!" Willa exclaimed suddenly. Baz's head popped up from a bush. She looked over, deadpan.

"Fascinating." And she dropped into the bush again.

Willa stripped down to her new bathing suit, eased into the pool, and swam down for a closer look. The vine was indeed growing out of the smaller time hole. She tugged on it. It was firmly attached.

Just then there was a sploosh, and Belle was in the water too, her pale skin glistening and fish tail curling gracefully behind her. Swimming naked didn't seem to faze her in the least. Willa wished she could be as unself-conscious as Belle.

Willa pointed to the vine in the time hole, but Belle shook her head, pointing instead to the larger time hole. They swam over to it and looked it over. Then Belle turned to Willa, holding out her hand. Willa took it, and together they swam into the silvery bubble.

They entered the dark tunnel and swam toward the spot of light at the other end. Gripping Belle's hand, Willa could barely contain her excitement to be down here with her. Every so often they'd sail past a large mirror on the wall, and Willa would catch a glimpse of Belle's long silver hair streaming out behind them, and herself being pulled along, pale and wide-eyed. It seemed to Willa that Belle's image in the mirrors looked younger and slimmer the further they swam.

They came to a stop. The round portal was now in front of them, and Belle turned to her.

Remember, we're not going out. We're just taking a look.

Willa nodded. They slipped their heads through the disc and looked out.

The sun was low behind a desert landscape. Figures in long white robes trudged by, while others rode camels. Women carried large jugs on their heads. Everyone seemed to be heading toward a collection of tents in the distance. To their left, something very large loomed. Willa looked up at it and let out a gasp.

It was the Great Sphinx, like she'd seen in history books, but with a difference: it still had a nose, and the face was smooth and serene, free from the ravages of time.

Willa turned to Belle, her eyes wide. *When is this?*

Belle smiled and shrugged. Willa looked at the people and tents with new interest. As the sun sank lower and the light faded, a long line of camels approached, also heading toward the tent city. Willa gazed at the billowing robes and scarves, the swaying motion of the animals, the slow way the people walked. Somewhere in the distance a voice rang out in a strange, chanting song, and Willa felt the thrill of being present in a distant, distant time.

When it was too dark to see anymore, they swam back and climbed out of the pool into the daylight of their own time. They didn't speak, but Willa gave Belle's hand a squeeze as she left. She walked home slowly, the swaying camels still in her mind.

The next day they went back through the same bubble but emerged in a different, even more incredible scene.

Before them was a marshy swamp, and a large dinosaur was lying in the reeds. Her awkwardly long neck and small head reminded Willa of Dinah, only this dinosaur had stripy markings on her legs. A baby dinosaur flopped around in the shallow water beside her. Willa stared, transfixed. Enormous dragonflies buzzed lazily overhead, and the sun beat down. The mother dinosaur's eyelids drooped, and she laid her head down for a nap.

When the baby realized she was asleep, it looked around and spotted them. Willa froze, her heart beating loudly as the little dinosaur approached, snuffling cautiously. It came closer and closer until they were practically nose-to-nose with Willa staring into its soft brown eyes.

"Just like Dinah," said Willa. "Look at her eyelashes!"

"Shoo! Go!" Belle hissed. "We don't want your mama after us. Shoo!" Belle waved her hand, but the little beast just head-butted her palm.

At that moment a shadow passed overhead and something very large dropped from the sky, its claws reaching out for the baby dinosaur.

Without thinking, Willa threw her arms around the dinosaur's neck and pulled it partially inside the time hole, knocking Belle, cursing, back into the tunnel. The pterodactyl missed its prey, hitting the water feet-first.

"Watch what you're doing!" hollered Belle.

The mother dinosaur let out a bellow as she lurched to her feet. The pterodactyl struggled to lift off from the water, finally taking to the sky with an angry squawk.

Willa hurriedly pushed the baby back out into the water, and it paddled over to its mother.

"What were you thinking?" grumbled Belle as she rejoined Willa.

"I couldn't let her be killed!" answered Willa.

Belle clucked her tongue. "Let's get out of here before something else happens."

Willa waved goodbye, and the baby dinosaur watched them disappear from sight.

Back in their own pool, Belle was still shaking her head.

"We're just there to look, not to be heroes!" she muttered.

Willa smiled. "I don't care, I'm glad I helped her out."

"I don't know anything about changing stuff in the past," Belle said with a worried look. "That might have been a really bad move."

Willa considered this for a moment. "I don't think so. I have a strong hunch it was the right thing to do."

Rustling and faint whispers. The brush of leaves on her face. Willa opened her eyes. She was swimming through green again, swimming toward the leafy face, staring into the grey eyes. Once again she sent out her question—

Who are you?

Again the mouth opened and the vines burst out, sweeping Willa along backward. She somersaulted through the foliage, growing weaker as she went. The light began to fade, and she was filled with despair. Then the violet eyes appeared ahead of her, looking curiously at her.

What have we here then? they said.

Willa smiled, and she felt her sadness fall away. The eyes disappeared, and Willa struggled against the tide with renewed strength. She threw both arms around a thick vine, which pulled her along at a tremendous pace until it shot up into the open air, and all was quiet.

Willa hugged the vine as it rose into the air. All around her, as far as the eye could see, was an ocean of greenery, and still they rose, up into the white fuzz of a cloud....

Willa opened her eyes and took in the familiar confines of her bedroom.

Another weird one, she thought. *These plant dreams are starting to get a little old.*

Chapter Eighteen

Violet eyes

The next day, Willa found Argus in the main hall, listening at Miss Trang's door. He put his finger to his lips and led Willa into the parlour.

"Miss Trang is stirring," he told her. "I heard her talking in her sleep. I think she'll be waking up soon."

"What?" Oberon launched himself from his carriage. "The demon dragon awakes?" His rabbits, who were forever lounging about the parlour, sat up with their noses twitching, suddenly alert.

Robert looked up from his book. "She's not a 'demon dragon,' you nitwit."

"She's really quite nice," added Willa. "You'll see."

"*Nice?*" Oberon was beside himself. "She nearly *incinerated* me the day I arrived! Don't you remember?" He looked to the rabbits, and they nodded hastily. There was a snort from above.

Mab sat in her doorway, clearly amused. "She was nowhere near you!"

"I could have been killed!" insisted Oberon.

"Mab's right. You were all the way across the room," said Willa with growing irritation. "Behind the sofa, covered in dust."

Oberon drew himself up to look very nearly kingly. "She is, nonetheless, a fire-breathing dragon, and in the interest of the safety of my court and my Royal Self, I demand that she take residence elsewhere!"

Mab jumped to her feet but Willa beat her to the punch. "If anyone is going to move out, it's going to be *Your* Royal Self!" she exploded. "How dare you come in here and start evicting people! Miss Trang is a member of this household, and you are not!"

Oberon was speechless. Robert began to applaud, and Argus smiled into his hand. Mab was laughing so hard, she fell backward into her nest. Oberon retreated into his golden carriage, sputtering with indignation. The rabbits glared at Willa. She decided it was a good time to go for a swim.

Belle was taking a nap, however, and Willa decided not to wake her. She wanted to go through a time hole on her own this time. She swam down to the bubbles, once again inspecting the vine coming out of the smaller one and giving it a tug. It was firmly anchored, that seemed clear. What was to stop her from just pulling herself, hand over hand, along it?

She reached in, grasped the vine, and with a thrill of excitement slipped through the bubble. This was a much smaller tunnel, barely big enough for her to wiggle through. It was good to have the vine to pull herself along, since it was hard to swim in such a constricted space. The walls of the tunnel were slippery and cold to the touch. She hesitated more than once, wondering if this was such a good idea, but she was encouraged by the presence of the vine and kept going.

She was relieved to finally spot light ahead. The tunnel curved upward right at the end, and she slipped her head through the disc into bright daylight.

Once her eyes adjusted, she realized she was in a large stone well. Keeping one hand on the vine, she felt the sides. The stone was smooth and cold, the same as the walls of the tunnel.

There was nothing else to do but pull herself up and look out. The level of the water was quite high in the well, so she didn't have to raise herself very far. She was careful to keep her legs inside the bubble, so she didn't feel it was too risky a move.

The well was in the middle of a forest clearing. A short distance away stood a simple hut with a thatched straw roof. A goat was tied to a stake outside, gazing sleepily at her. A rough broom, a stool, and a few simple iron tools lay around, and bundles of herbs had been hung on the walls to dry. There was also a large sword leaning against the wall.

Real fairy tale–style, she thought excitedly. *Am I in medieval times?*

A young girl came out of the hut with a fat cat padding along at her heels. Willa ducked down but continued to peek out over the edge of the well. The girl took down several bundles of herbs and began tying them together with twine. She had a wild mass of black hair and wore a rough woollen tunic over leggings and leather slippers. She looked the same age as Willa, or maybe a year younger. She was small and slight but moved about like she owned the place and wore a very determined expression.

Just then a small, ugly man crept out of the bushes and snuck up to the goat, who was around the corner of the hut and out of sight of the girl. Willa had never seen anything like him. His arms reached the ground, his skin was pale with a greenish tinge, and he was dressed in filthy leather garments. He reached stealthily for the rope around the goat's neck. Though he was being perfectly silent, the girl suddenly stopped, listening. She shook her head in irritation and held out her hands with the palms upward. As she stared intently, a whirling ball of black smoke began to form above them.

Willa blinked. *Now that's interesting.*

When the smoke had grown to the size of a soccer ball, the girl threw it. The smoke curved neatly around the corner and hit the little man in the face. He staggered back, spluttering, and when the smoke cleared, his face was covered in soot.

"Get away wi' ye, ugly wart of a goblin!" hollered the girl as she walked up. "Ye'll not be gettin' my goat today, or any other day!"

The goblin fled into the trees, and Willa decided she liked this strange girl. The girl gave her goat a quick hug and looked around.

"Where have ye gone, Loom? It's time we made our deliveries," she called out.

Willa ducked out of sight as the girl looked her way. Then she heard a *meow*, and a cat's face appeared in the opening of the well, looking down at her. It was a mangy old black cat with half of one ear missing and fringes of grey around its eyes like shaggy eyebrows.

"What is it, Loom?" asked the girl, her face appearing next to the cat's, and she looked down at Willa with wide-set, brilliant violet eyes.

What have we here then? The message came loud and clear into Willa's mind as she stared back with a shock of recognition. Unmistakable. Those were the eyes she had seen in her dreams. She felt for a moment that she might be dreaming again.

The girl frowned. "Do I know ye?"

"No," answered Willa. "I don't think so."

The strange girl bit her lip thoughtfully. "Did you steal me bucket?"

"Um, no."

"What about granting wishes? Are ye a pixie?"

"No, I'm not magic at all. My name's Willa. What's your name?"

"Gwyneth," the girl answered. "If you're not magic, how do ye happen to pop out of a holy well?"

"I don't know," admitted Willa. "It was just an accident me coming out here. Is it really holy?"

Gwyneth nodded vigorously. "Aye, for hundreds of years! And it's my family that's been looking after it all that time." Something small appeared on the top of her head, looking out sleepily from the tangle of black hair. Willa was surprised to see it was a fairy.

"Look, Hawthorn," said Gwyneth matter-of-factly. "See what Loom found in the well." The fairy whispered into Gwyneth's ear.

"Nay," the girl guffawed. "I dinna conjure her. I'm not that good yet." The cat snorted.

"Are you a magician?" asked Willa.

"Nay," said Gwyneth. "I'm a witch."

Willa looked at her with new admiration. "That is so cool."

Gwyneth gave her a funny look. "Em, what?"

"It's impressive, I mean."

"'Tis just a job," shrugged Gwyneth, giving Willa another long, hard stare. "I canna help but think I've met ye before somewhere." Her face softened into a smile. "And I've a funny feelin' we're friends."

Willa smiled back. She wanted to tell her about the dreams but thought it would be too weird.

Then Gwyneth sighed and shook her head. "I'd love to set an' figure it out, but I've got to be gettin' back to work. You're welcome to come and visit, Willa, anytime at all." She started back toward her hut.

"Thank you," said Willa. She watched Gwyneth slip the large sword into a sheath hanging from her belt and gather up her bundle of herbs.

As she marched off into the trees, Gwyneth called back over her shoulder, "Come for Beltane, 'twill be a lively time!" Then she disappeared into the woods. Her cat followed, looking back at Willa with its tail curled into a question mark.

Willa descended into the darkness and started back.

She really liked this strange girl. So strong and confident. And brave!

Her eyes are the eyes from my dream, that's for sure. But what does it all mean? It was only then that she remembered about time holes drifting and realized she wouldn't be able to return. Her eyes filled with tears. Considering she'd only talked to Gwyneth for a couple of minutes, she was surprised at how sad she felt. It was like she'd discovered a long-lost friend, or even a sister, only to lose her again.

Chapter Nineteen

Mermaids and remorse

The next day, Willa joined Argus on the front porch. She felt a little guilty for shouting at Oberon and asked Argus if the fairy king was still angry with her.

"I don't think so. He's actually quite cheerful today. I'm not sure why, unless it's because he's made friends with the spider."

"Tabitha?" asked Willa in surprise. "I thought he was scared to death of her."

"I saw her talking to him after your little argument yesterday. They had a nice long chat and have been on good terms ever since."

"That's good, I guess," Willa said. "What did they talk about?"

Argus looked hurt. "I draw the line at eavesdropping," he said. "Very unprofessional."

"All right. What does Mab think about this new friendship?"

"She was furious at first, but Oberon's fairies are building something in secret." Argus led her into the parlour. In a corner of the room, what looked like a small circus tent covered an end table. From within came the sound of hammering and sawing.

Argus lowered his voice to a whisper. "Mab's certain it's a surprise present for her, so she's not quite so angry with him."

Willa winced. "Why does that just make me more worried?"

Argus smiled. "Because every time a problem is solved around here, three new ones pop up?"

"Yep," said Willa with a sigh.

Belle was already in the pool waiting for her. "Hurry up!" she urged. "The time hole is lined up perfectly today! Hurry!"

Willa had planned to tell her about Gwyneth, but Belle was off like a shot, leading the way to the larger bubble. They plunged together into the dark corridor.

When they reached the other side, Willa looked out into a round room with a vast vaulted ceiling of stained glass, through which a pale light shone. The arching walls were gold, carved with elegant patterns. In the centre of the room was a sparkling fountain, above which floated a large glowing orb with hundreds of tiny fish swimming in and out of it.

Willa stared in wonder at the dazzling sight, then at Belle, who suddenly looked about twenty years younger. Belle swung her tail around and sat on the edge of the portal, so Willa did the same, dangling her feet.

Then there was a sudden rush as a dozen lithe mermaids crowded around them. They stared at Willa with immense eyes, and though they didn't speak out loud, she could hear their excited chatter in her head.

What's this? Who is it? I saw them first! Who is she? What is she? Look at her!

Willa felt a sudden embarrassment about having legs. Smiling, Belle put her arm around Willa's shoulders.

This is my granddaughter. Willa felt reassured and proud as the mermaids reached out to touch her and run their fingers through her hair.

After a while the mermaids lost interest in them and scooted about the room, playing games, chasing and dodging each other. Then they slipped away, one by one, until Willa and Belle were left alone. Belle took her hand, and they swam back down the dark corridor.

Gliding by the mirrors, Willa marvelled at her own reflection each time. *Is that me? Is it really, really me? Could I really belong with them, in that amazing place?*

Emerging from the time hole, the pool water seemed murky and uninteresting. Willa rose to the surface with a sigh.

Belle eyed her happily. "Just a little taste of my old home," she said. "What do you think?"

"Oh, Belle," gushed Willa without thinking. "Why did you leave? It's so beautiful!"

Belle's face grew solemn. "I was restless. I couldn't help but go back and forth between the sea and the world." Then she smiled. "Humans can be pretty interesting."

"So you went back and forth," prompted Willa. "And then?"

"You can't keep that up for too long before it starts taking its toll on your body. For a long while I lost the ability to breath underwater." Belle paused, gazing into the distance. Then she went on, shaking her head at the memory. "Horrible. I got it back, thankfully, but breathing air for so long caused my body to change, and now my heart can't take the deep sea pressure." She flipped her tail in the water, splashing Willa. "Nice place to visit, but I can't live there."

Willa helped her out of the pool and into her robe and chair. "Is that so bad?" she finally asked.

"Not so bad," smiled Belle, and they went inside.

Then came another weekend. Willa woke up Saturday morning thinking about water. The craving was even worse than the weekend before. Swimming was all she could think about. She took a bath on Saturday morning, and when her mom went out to a hair appointment in the afternoon, she took another bath. She knew her dad wouldn't notice she was in the tub again, and she was right.

After dinner she tried to think of a reason to take yet another bath, but she couldn't. Instead, she filled a large mixing bowl with water and snuck it into her room, where she periodically plunged her face into it.

I am such a weirdo, she mused.

On Sunday they visited Grandpa. As they sat in his beachfront bungalow, the sound of waves nearly drove Willa mad. She took a long, long walk on the beach by herself, and stared out at the surf. A swimming pool was one thing, but the ocean? What would it be like to swim out there? Was she really over her fear? She dug down deep but couldn't find the old terror. It seemed to have been replaced by a new tingling, restless excitement. Pulling off her rubber boots and socks, she stood barefoot in the water and wiggled her toes in the sand.

It doesn't make sense. Phobias don't disappear like that. They don't vanish without a trace.

How did she become afraid of the water in the first place? Was it just because her mom was always warning her about it? Had she picked up her mom's fear somehow?

She stared at the water. Each time the waves receded she could feel them pulling her, and she waded deeper, following the water out....

"Willa! Time to go home!" her dad called.

Willa jumped guiltily, grabbed her boots, and sprinted back to the house. That night at home she took another bath, an extra long one. Her mom knocked once to make sure she was all right, and when Willa emerged in her robe, her mom gave her a long, hard look.

"Are you all right?" she asked.

"Yeah, why?" Willa sauntered casually to her room. She knew her cocky attitude would drive her mom nuts, but she was carried forward on a wave of pride. And guilt.

I am lying to her. She has a right to be suspicious.

But I've got a right to my privacy. She doesn't need to know where I am every minute of the day.

You are swimming! That is huge. You have to tell her.

If she was more reasonable, I'd tell her. But she's not, and I don't need her flipping out on me again.

150

Her thoughts countered each other, back and forth. She went to bed early just so the mental debate would end. Her busy brain finally settled on one happy thought:

Tomorrow I'll go for a swim!

Chapter Twenty

A surprising return

After the longest weekend of her life and the longest Monday at school, Willa fairly sprinted to Eldritch Manor. The sun peeked through ragged clouds, and the air was warm. She found Argus sitting on the porch.

"Hi, Argus. Did you see? The third floor is started!" exclaimed Willa, joining him. The second floor looked pretty much complete, and above it the white beams were starting to outline the third floor.

Argus just grunted. His chin rested in his hand, and he looked wearier than usual.

"What's up?"

"Old age, Willa. It's no fun. I've got aches in my joints, arthritis, back pain. Even worse, some of my eyes are acting up! My vision's been blurry all weekend. I think I'm getting cataracts."

"You should see an eye doctor," Willa said without thinking. Argus raised an eyebrow. "Or not." Willa smiled. "But at least you've got extra eyes for backup."

That didn't seem to cheer him up much.

Darkling Green

"Would you like me to take a look? Which eyes are blurry?"

"Mostly in the back," answered Argus. He turned, pointing to the eyes on the back of his neck and skull. Willa stepped closer. Right away she could see that they were obscured by fine white strands, hundreds of them crisscrossing each eye.

"The only thing wrong with your eyes is that they're covered with something," she told him. "Have you got a handkerchief?"

Argus handed her a hankie, and Willa carefully cleared away the fuzzy white strands. Once cleared, the eyes blinked and stared at her. Willa shivered.

"Much better! Thank you, Willa," exclaimed Argus. "What was covering them?"

Willa showed him the hankie. "Tiny threads. Almost like cobwebs."

Argus looked perplexed. "Hmm."

Willa moved toward the steps. "Well, I was just going to go for a swim."

"Wait, I'll give you my report." Argus rubbed his forehead thoughtfully. "Eldritch Manor surveillance report, April nineteenth. Um. Let's see. Miss Trang hasn't woken yet. I haven't heard a peep from her all weekend. Horace and Tengu are still shut up with the basilisk. The fairies had another party, lutes and harps playing until dawn. Drove me crazy. Baz ate a scorpion this morning, but it doesn't seem to have affected her. I think she's got a cast-iron stomach."

"Great. Thanks, Argus." Willa edged down the steps, eager to go.

"Baz is also going on and on about someone messing around in her room yesterday. I didn't see anyone go in there, but with my eyes mucked up I wasn't really at my best…."

He looked so glum that Willa patted him on the back (doing her best to avoid poking any eyes). "Don't worry, Argus. You're doing a wonderful job. Now if you'll excuse me, I'm just going to—" She started to move again.

"And …"

"Yes?"

"We're out of milk," Argus said sadly. "No milk for tea."

"Tell Baz, she's the one who buys the groceries."

"She says she's too busy."

Willa smiled. "Okay, I'll run and get some."

She hurried to the corner store and returned with the milk, which she handed to Argus. "Make yourself some tea. I'm just going to go for a swim—"

CRASH! Willa jumped as thunder shook the whole neighbourhood. The heavens opened, and rain poured down. She and Argus exchanged surprised looks.

"Mab," they both said together.

They heard shouting as soon as they opened the door. The air was so electric, Willa got a huge shock from the doorknob. The parlour lights were flickering, and there was a furious hum as Mab flew around and around in circles, shooting sparks in all directions. The rabbits stood on guard in front of the end table. The tent-like covering was gone, revealing a compact but elegant doll's house, an old-fashioned mansion with pillars in front.

"Mab! Mab! What's wrong?" Willa shouted.

The blur came to a standstill, and Mab appeared in sharp focus, all jagged edges, with wild hair and wilder eyes. She began to squeal at such a high pitch that Willa could barely hear it. Argus leaned in to listen.

"Something about the dollhouse, but I can't quite make it out," he said finally. "She's reaching frequencies that only dogs can hear properly."

"What's wrong with the dollhouse? I think it's beautiful," said Willa.

Mab howled in rage, then began squealing again. Argus listened, finally grimacing.

"What's wrong?" asked Willa.

"The dollhouse," he explained sadly, "is not for Mab. Oberon had it built for Tabitha."

Mab flew to the front of the house, but the rabbits closed ranks to keep her from reaching it. She began zapping them, and they cowered behind their shields.

"Mab! Stop it at once!" came Oberon's sharp voice from behind them.

Willa turned to see Oberon in the doorway, riding on Tabitha's back. He slid to the ground, and the rabbits snapped to attention. Tabitha scuttled between them and began clambering into the dollhouse through a large front window.

"Wait, Tabitha," called Willa.

The spider paused in the window and looked up brightly. "Yes, darlin'?"

Willa held out Argus's handkerchief. "I need your expertise. What do you think these are? Are they spider-made?"

Tabitha peered closely at the strands with her big eyes, tutting disapprovingly. "Hmm. Very crude work. Definitely not spider. Coccoon silk from a caterpillar, maybe?"

They were interrupted by a new ruckus. Mab was shooting sparks at Oberon, who took refuge in a teacup on the coffee table. Willa dashed between them, and Mab zapped her in the kneecap.

"Ouch! Stop it, Mab!"

Mab hung back. Oberon peeked over the rim of the teacup and stuck out his tongue. Mab growled. Smoke rose from her head.

"Oberon, why did you make a house for Tabitha?" asked Willa.

"Because she needed one. She can't live in a *bowl* all the time!" he answered.

"She should be up there knitting!" hissed Mab.

"Dearest, she's way ahead on the scarf. Have you even looked at it recently?" countered Oberon.

Willa peeked into the hanging bowl, which indeed was full of coiled scarf.

"It's true. Look at it all!" Willa held up a handful. "This should last us the rest of the month. Tabitha deserves a holiday, don't you think, Mab?" Before she even turned around, Mab had whizzed up into her wasp nest and slammed the door. Willa ran the scarf through her fingers, admiring the leafy pattern once again. As she turned it in the light, however, a new detail was revealed.

Eyes looked out from between the leaves, but Willa could only see them with the scarf turned one way. She had a quick flash of her repetitive dreams, the face in the leaves, the grey eyes….

Tabitha had disappeared inside the dollhouse, and the rabbits were barring the way, shoulder-to-shoulder with swords and shields in front.

"I need to talk to Tabitha, if you don't mind," Willa said firmly. The rabbits eyed Oberon, now reclining on a cushion. He shook his head.

"Madame Tabitha is not seeing anyone today."

"But I was just talking to her!" protested Willa. "Why are you two suddenly such best friends?"

Oberon shrugged, looking intensely bored. The rabbits stared at her coldly. Willa felt a sudden urge to be swimming, but it was too late now. With a deep sigh she left the house and turned toward home.

The next day it was still pouring rain. She didn't go into the house for fear of more turmoil delaying her swim.

Willa shivered a little as she slipped into the dark water. She swam down and circled the bottom, looking at both time holes, deciding on the smaller one once more. *Might as well see where it leads today.* She gripped the vine once more and pulled herself through the same cold, slippery space.

At the other end she found herself enclosed in circular stone walls. Her heart leapt. *The well? I'm back in the well!*

She pulled herself up and looked out. Sure enough, it was the same well in the same place. The hut was there, and the goat. Gwyneth's cat lay sleeping in the sunshine. Willa stared at the scene in shock.

It's exactly the same place and time. But how can that be? The time hole hasn't shifted in five days. Is that possible?

The cat looked at her. He jumped up and trotted around the side of the hut, returning in a few moments with the black-haired girl. She held a thin black rope in her hand, attached to something shiny that banged on the ground behind her.

"Good morrow to ye," she said, hopping up to sit on the side of the well. "How are things in the well today?"

"I don't actually live in here," said Willa, grinning happily. "I come from another land. In the future. I think." She was elated with the wonder of it all, with being here, chatting again with this girl from another time. Willa pointed to the bubble around her middle. "My world is connected to yours by this. It's a time hole."

The cat mewed loudly, and his eyes narrowed. Gwyneth turned back to Willa. "Loom says that's impossible. He says time holes dinna stay in one place. They move around."

"Usually they do, but this one seems special for some reason," replied Willa.

Gwyneth turned to the cat again, annoyed. "Why haven't ye taught me 'bout time holes?" The cat mewed back, and Gwyneth sighed. "Says I'm not ready for them."

"He's teaching you?"

"Of course. He's teachin' me the witchin' arts. I wouldn't be gettin' very far on my own now, would I?"

Willa considered this. "Is magic pretty common here?"

"What do you mean?"

"Can everyone do magic?"

"Nay, but there are plenty of us who can. An' there's no end of work to do. The dark is all around, you know."

"The dark?"

"Aye. We're battlin' it all th' time, that's why we're needin' all the witches we can train."

"I've only come face-to-face with the dark side a couple of times. It seems to have a lot of trouble breaking through to my world."

Gwyneth laughed. "Sounds dead boring. I enjoy a good fight." She pointed to the vine. "What do ye know about this?"

"Not very much, I'm afraid, other than it goes all the way through to my world. And it grows really fast."

"It sprouted up over that way." Gwyneth gestured toward the woods. "Grew straight on toward the well, and then into it. We're not sure what it is, exactly, but we're keepin' an eye on it."

"Sorry I can't tell you any more," said Willa, then she looked her in the eyes and thought—

You can send messages like this, can't you?

Gwyneth grinned. *Since I was a young 'un. Easy as porridge.*

I've only just learned how.

Are ye human or elf?

Human … and mermaid.

That makes sense. I'm half elfling on my ma's side.

Do you live on your own here?

Aye, since I was seven. My ma and pa were killed fightin' mountain trolls.

I'm so sorry.

Gwyneth looked at her brightly. *Oh, it's all right. I've got everythin' I'm needin', and the villagers are grand. Lots of excitement, lots to do.*

Then she squinted thoughtfully at Willa and muttered to herself. "Ye look so familiar." Loom meowed loudly and pawed at Gwyneth's leg.

"Oh, all right. I've got to go," said Gwyneth, jumping down. "Loom needs his dinner." As she started away Willa got a better look at the shiny thing she was dragging behind her.

"Wait," said Willa, staring. "Where did you get that?"

Gwyneth raised the black cord, and the shiny metal box dangled in front of her. "I found it floatin' in the well a while back. I think it's some manner of weapon. Watch!" Gwyneth swung it in circles above her head and then whipped it around a nearby tree. As the box circled the trunk, Gwyneth performed two rapid loops around it with the cord and pulled it tight, exactly like a cowboy might rope a steer.

"Nice," said Willa with a smile. "But it's not a weapon. It's a toaster."

"You mean for makin' toast? I should think a sharp stick would work much better!" Gwyneth unlooped the cord and swung the toaster neatly into her hand. "Come along, Loom. Fare thee well, Willa!" She strode away and then called over her shoulder. "Keep an eye out for me bucket down there, will ye?"

"Sure, bye!"

Willa lowered herself into the well, lost in thought. *That looks like our toaster. The one that fell into the time hole when it went through the house. And her missing bucket is probably the one Tengu found that night too.*

She moved through the dark tunnel, her thoughts in a whirl.

Which means this time hole has connected us to the holy well from the very beginning!

Chapter Twenty-One

The man of Darkling Green

When Willa emerged at the other end, the rain had stopped. She floated on her back for a while, thinking. She'd have to ask Horace about this. Maybe the holy well was a time wrinkle too, just like their pool. If this time hole was actually stuck at both ends, it could very well be a permanent passageway to the Middle Ages and her new friend, Gwyneth the witch. Willa grinned from ear to ear.

She gazed at the woods beyond the pool. The upper canopy was so dense, it completely blocked the light. A closer look revealed that the denseness was due to vines, clinging and growing up the tree trunks and filling in the forest ceiling. Willa suddenly remembered the mass of vines at the back wall. She climbed out of the pool, dried herself off, and made her way through the dark and gloomy woods.

The wall was now so completely covered that it looked like it was made of leaves. There was a figure there in the dark, and she nearly jumped out of her skin before realizing it was just the cluster of vines she'd seen before, grown larger. It looked uncannily like a large man sitting with his back against the wall, his head bowed forward as if asleep. It was like those specially trimmed bushes you sometimes see in gardens, trimmed into the shapes of animals and birds. Willa walked around it, observing it from all sides. It was so lifelike that the chest and shoulders even seemed to rise and fall with breath.

It's because of the breeze, Willa told herself, but she backed away quietly, afraid to disturb it.

The next day Willa knocked on Tengu's door. They were hard at work, Horace madly scribbling notes while Tengu barked commands to the blindfolded basilisk.

"Two steps to the left … one step forward … three steps backward…."

To Willa's amazement, the basilisk was following his instructions to the letter. Tengu let out a low whistle, and the creature jumped meekly onto his shoulder.

"Say hello to Willa. She is a friend."

The basilisk nodded twice and squawked.

"That is amazing!" exclaimed Willa.

"The basilisk has a tremendous aptitude for language acquisition," Horace enthused. He pointed to reams of handwritten notes. "I'm documenting everything for publication. We've entered uncharted territory, scientifically speaking."

"What about the blindfold? Are you still planning to take it off?"

Tengu and Horace exchanged nervous looks. Finally Horace answered, "Not quite yet."

"I've got something else that might interest you, about the time wrinkle in our pool…." Willa stopped.

"Hmm? What pool?" Horace looked up at her, and there was an odd blankness in his eye that she knew well. *His memory is slipping again.* "Never mind, I'll tell you later. Tengu, do you still have the bucket that fell out of the time hole?"

He nodded.

"Can I have it, please?"

Willa pulled herself through the small time hole once more, the bucket handle looped over one arm. She was fairly certain she'd come out in the well again, but she was nervous all the same. Her head popped out of the water, and her heart leaped to see the familiar stone walls.

It was darker this time, she guessed early evening. There was no light or sign of life in the hut. Willa lifted the bucket up onto the edge of the well and rested there a moment, drinking in the peaceful scene.

Her thoughts were interrupted by the sound of hooves. She waited and watched. In the fading light she saw a white shape emerge from the trees. Willa squinted, doubting her own eyes. It was a large white horse with a long white horn.

Holy moley! It's a unicorn!

Trembling with excitement, Willa watched him approach the well, unconcerned about her presence. He sniffed her and snorted softly. Willa shifted to the side to make room for him to drink from the well.

Then the unicorn noticed the vine and sniffed at it, growing more and more agitated. With his nose to the ground, he began to follow the vine toward the trees.

Willa pulled herself up a little higher, even daring to pull her feet right out of the water. She sat on the edge of the well and looked down at the silvery bubble with her reflection in the middle of it.

It's not going anywhere. It hasn't budged in a whole month.

She swung her legs over the side, dropped to the ground, and hurried after the unicorn. A short distance into the woods, the unicorn stopped. Willa had to step around him, and what she saw made her catch her breath.

In front of her was a mass of vines grown up into the shape of a seated person, its head bowed, identical to the figure at Eldritch Manor.

Willa felt the unicorn's nose pushing at her, and she turned away from the figure. They walked together back to the well. She ran her hand down his nose and he turned to leave.

Goodbye, she thought.

Be careful, came the reply as the unicorn plodded away.

Wait! Be careful of what? Willa asked as he disappeared into the woods. There was no answer. She stayed a while longer, lost in thought. She wished Gwyneth was there to talk to, but it was obvious she was out, so Willa climbed back into the well.

She found Belle in her chair at the edge of the pool, yawning. "Sorry. I was napping. The days are just so long!"

"Belle!" exclaimed Willa. "I saw a unicorn!"

"That's nice," Belle answered, handing her a towel.

Willa pulled herself out of the pool. "I went through the smaller time hole. It always ends in the same place and the same time."

"Nonsense," said Belle. "Time holes don't work that way."

"This one does," said Willa. "It goes to a holy well in medieval times, and I met a girl there who's a witch. And the vines there are growing in the shape of a person, just the same as here…." She trailed off.

"Mm-hmm," Belle said with another yawn.

Willa looked at her carefully. "Are you angry at me for going without you?"

Belle laughed. "Nope. That's called freedom, kiddo. Enjoy it! You can't get that at home, can you?"

"I guess not."

"It's a crying shame. Human beings are so tied down with the cares of the world that they don't even know what freedom is. They're scared of it."

Willa started to pull her clothes on. She hadn't thought of it like that before. Swimming did feel like freedom.

"It's the same here," she observed. "I can't walk two steps in the door without hearing about everybody's problems."

Belle burst into laughter. "That's right, that's right. Everyone's trying to tie you up, pull you down. When it gets to be too much, you've just got to …" Here she held up her hands, palms together, and pulled them apart, "… detach."

Willa suddenly thought of Belle leaving Grandpa and her mom. Detach. Simple as that.

"Sure. Detach." Willa's voice was cold. Belle looked at her quizzically, but Willa didn't say anything more. She just packed her bag and walked away.

Grey eyes fringed with leaves. The solemn mouth. Willa stared into the face once more. She was just about to ask her question when the leaves shifted and the mouth opened. The leaves parted to reveal a great black space beyond, and the mouth formed words that Willa felt vibrating in her chest:

Who are you?

The question was directed at her this time. Willa opened her mouth to answer, but there was a tickling in her throat, and out of her mouth flowed vines, branches, leaves, and flowers, hitting the floor and pooling around her. Soon she was swimming in branches that scratched and tore at her skin. The surface of the greenery rippled, and a wave covered her face.

Chapter Twenty-Two

A tsunami of trouble

She wasn't able to visit Gwyneth the next day. Argus was waiting for her on the porch, his face drawn in worry.

"Come. Hurry," was all he said, leading her to Miss Trang's room. Horace, Baz, Belle, Mab, Tengu, Robert, and Mjodvitnir were all there and all looking anxious. Miss Trang lay in bed, still asleep, the sound of her raspy breathing filling the room. All dragon traces were gone. She looked very human, and very ill. Her skin was yellow, and her face was beaded with sweat, even though she was shivering. Horace held her wrist, taking her pulse.

"What's wrong with her?" whispered Willa.

"We don't know," answered Argus. "A few days ago she looked fine, like she was about to wake up, and now …" He gestured helplessly.

"Should we call a doctor?" asked Willa.

Horace tucked Miss Trang's hand under the covers. "Your doctors couldn't help here," he said. "Dragon physiognomy and all. Besides, I don't think it's a simple illness."

"Why not?"

"She's not a simple patient."

Willa looked at her sadly. "I suppose not."

Horace began ushering everyone out of the room. "We'll take turns watching her, and hopefully whatever it is will pass. Maybe it's just some kind of dragon flu."

In the hall, Willa felt something underfoot and was surprised to see a plant sprouting up between the floorboards.

"Look." She pointed at the sprout. "Where is this coming from?"

Mjodvitnir opened the ramp. The basement was still under a few inches of water, and the walls were fuzzy and green.

Robert cursed. "Moss! My room is covered in stinking moss!"

Not only that, but over top of the moss were leafy vines growing up the walls. They disappeared into the ceiling, squeezing between the boards. Mjodvitnir shook his head.

"This is not normal. Those plants are not of this world."

"That could be," said Willa. "And I know where they're coming from."

She led Horace, Robert, and Mjodvitnir to the pool and brushed aside the green slurry that covered the surface so they could see beneath it.

"The time holes," she explained. "The two time holes that settled into the pool are both still down there and out of that one ..." she pointed, "... the smaller one, see it? There's a small vine growing out of it, and everything here is branching out from it."

Horace peered down, tracing the path with his finger. "That one vine … and now it's covering the forest floor…."

"Going all the way to the back wall…." added Willa.

"Up over the top of the trees," observed Robert. "And along the ground to the house."

Horace was lost in thought. "All this growth after just one month." He stepped forward to look into the pool again. "What do we know about that particular time hole?"

"That's the most interesting part," said Willa. "The big bubble always ends in a different place, it moves around like it's supposed to, but the small one always leads to the same time and place. It comes out in a holy well in the middle ages, where there are unicorns and fairies and witches and things like that."

"A holy well," muttered Horace.

"Could the well be a time wrinkle too? Like our pool? Could both ends of this time hole be stuck in place?" suggested Willa with great excitement.

Horace ran both hands through his hair. He had a bewildered look about him. "I've never heard anything like it. I suppose it's possible, but highly unlikely."

Meanwhile, Mjodvitnir and a couple other dwarves had armed themselves with axes and had begun hacking at the vines around the foundation of the house.

The daylight around them suddenly diminished. Willa looked at her watch and started. The hands were in motion, doing a slow spin around the dial, and it was already coming up to six o'clock.

"What? Time's moving fast now!" Willa showed Horace her watch. "What is Tabitha doing? My mom's going to kill me!"

Both of her parents were at the door as she ran up, out of breath. She'd concocted an alibi during her run home. It wasn't great, but it would have to do.

"I was studying in the library, and I fell asleep," she blurted out before her mom started yelling.

They both seemed to accept it, but her mom had a suspicious eye on her as they ate supper. Willa was just glad she hadn't been swimming and her hair wasn't wet.

Grey eyes fringed with leaves. The serious mouth. Willa stared at the face. *Again and again and again!* she thought. The mouth opened to the black space beyond, and it asked her:

Who are you?

Willa opened her mouth to answer, and out of her mouth flowed vines, branches, leaves, and flowers, pouring out, rising up until she was swimming in them. A wave covered her face. She closed her eyes to the green and felt herself falling.

Then a sound, a repetitive *clop clop clop clop*.

She opened her eyes. The unicorn was beside her. She pulled herself up onto his back and hugged his neck as they plunged through the leaves and vines. She closed her eyes, and after a while she had the sensation that she was walking.

She opened her eyes. She was walking down a city street. The clip-clopping continued beside her, but when she turned she didn't see the unicorn, she saw a black horse, walking upright on two legs like a man. She looked up at this familiar apparition, unafraid. They walked along together for a while.

You always come to warn me, she thought.

Yes.

And here you are again.

Yes.

She shivered and turned to face him. He was tall, and his eyes burned red.

Will Miss Trang be all right? she asked. *What should we do?*

The horse answered in slow, rhythmic verse. Willa strained to hear every word. Then the horse turned and ran, moving away from her at great speed but without making a sound. The silence pushed into her ears and exploded in her head.

Chapter Twenty-Three

In which Willa learns the whole truth

Willa woke with the remnants of a dream floating in her head, but they vanished as soon as she remembered poor Miss Trang.

I should have been paying more attention. I should have been checking on her.

She dressed in a hurry, hoping to duck out of the house before her mom got up.

No such luck. She was in the living room. Willa walked to the closet and got out her jacket, feeling her mother's eyes on her back.

"Where are you going on a Saturday morning?"

Willa took a deep breath before answering. "I have to go to Eldritch, Mom. It's an emergency. Miss Trang is very sick, she looks absolutely terrible, and I—"

"How do you know she looks terrible?"

Willa's heart sank. *Here we go.* "I was there yesterday."

"You said you were at the library."

"Yeah, well … "

"You lied to me. I told you not to go there, and you disobeyed me."

Willa flushed with anger. "I have a right to go where I want!"

"Back to your room."

"Miss Trang needs me. She's really sick!"

"The others can take care of her, I'm sure. The whole crazy house won't fall down without you! You need to learn that."

Willa stared at her in disbelief. Her mom had always been a hard case, stubborn and strict, but this was ridiculous. Willa turned and started out the door. As she stepped out onto the front step a single word crashed into her mind—

STOP!

The force of it nearly knocked her over. Willa steadied herself against the open door and stood there, recovering her thoughts. She turned and saw her mom with her hand over her mouth, her eyes wide.

"You ... you can do that?" gasped Willa. And then she knew the truth. She regarded her mother levelly. "I have a question for you."

Her mom had a frightened look in her eyes.

"Did you *make* me afraid of water?" Willa blurted out.

Her mom blinked. "How could I do that?"

"With mermaid powers. Putting ideas into my head, like you did just now!"

"Willa, don't— " started her mom.

"Did you give me that phobia? Did you brainwash me?" shot back Willa.

Her mom met her gaze, pale and trembling. "It was for your own good!" They stared at each other. Her mom sat heavily on the sofa, suddenly looking very small. "Willa …"

Willa slammed the door behind her and ran right into Grandpa on the front lawn.

"Hey, kiddo! What's the hurry?"

She looked at him, her eyes full of tears, then shook her head and ran off.

At Eldritch Manor, Willa paused in the front hall, wiping her eyes. Then she went to Miss Trang's room. Belle and Horace were there.

"How is she?"

"No change," said Horace.

Belle looked up at her tear-stained face. "Willa! What's wrong? What happened?"

Willa burst into tears as Belle led her into the parlour. "Mom, she … we had a fight." She sat down, and Belle took her hand.

"What did she do?"

"She … she was trying to keep me from coming here. And …" Willa stopped.

"And what?"

"Nothing. We just had a fight." She couldn't say it out loud. She couldn't say that her mom had messed with her mind when she was little. It was just too awful.

Belle gave Willa's hand a squeeze. "Stay here with us. We're your family now." Willa looked over at Robert, snoozing in the corner, and Baz, snoring on the couch.

"Lively bunch," she sniffed.

"We'll get a little supper into you, and you'll feel a lot better," said Belle.

"Supper? You mean breakfast."

"No, no. Look at the time. I'll see if there's any soup on."

Belle wheeled herself out of the room. Willa stood and tiptoed past Robert to look out the window.

For weeks, the outside world had been in slow-mo, but now the street was a blur of activity: people zooming back and forth, cars flashing by, clouds somersaulting across the sky.

Willa glanced again at the clock. She really didn't like the way the clock hands were marching along. She pulled over a stool and peeked into the knitting bowl. Tabitha wasn't there. Willa could see right away that the scarf had changed drastically: the stitches were now so long and stretched that the leafy pattern was distended and weird.

She lifted the scarf. Further along, the stitches grew even larger, and the yarn changed colour. The silver darkened slowly to a murky gun-metal grey. *That's not right*, thought Willa. Even the ball of yarn now looked nearly black. *What is Tabitha doing?*

She knocked on the dollhouse door, but there was no answer. Her thoughts were interrupted by Belle returning. "There'll be beef stew in a few minutes. Smells delicious."

Willa pointed to the clock. "Aren't you worried about the time zipping along like that?"

Belle shrugged. "Time marches on. When you're as old as I am, you don't pay so much attention to it." She rubbed her hands excitedly. "All right then. We'll have the dwarves whip up a room for you, and we'll have to find you some clothes…."

Willa sank into an armchair. "I should have packed a bag. I'll sneak home later and grab a few things."

Belle shook her head. "Better not take the chance. If she gets her claws into you, she won't let you leave again. Ever!"

Willa felt extremely weary. "Claws? She's not a monster."

"Don't be so sure," sniffed Belle.

"She may not be perfect, but she's still my mom," protested Willa. "The reason she acts like she does is because of you, you know."

Belle looked at her coldly. "I didn't do anything."

"You left her! That's really big for a kid."

"Mermaid children are fully independent by the age of two," Belle shot back.

Willa frowned. "Humans do things differently."

"You don't have to tell me." Belle rolled her eyes. "You don't understand how mermaids operate, sweetie." She pivoted her chair toward the doorway. "I'm going to see if I can't speed up that stew."

Belle rolled out of the room. Willa felt a sharp pain in her chest, like she was going to cry again.

"She is the way she is. You know that," said a calm voice. It was Baz, stretching and yawning herself awake on the sofa.

"Yeah, I know. She's a mermaid," Willa sighed.

Willa decided to go out to the pool to think, but as she opened the front door, she found herself face to face with Grandpa.

"Grandpa! What are you doing here?"

"Hi, kiddo." He gave her a wink. "Your mom sent me. She's kinda worried."

They sat on the front steps. Grandpa suddenly noticed that people and cars were just blurs. "Heavens! What's going on?"

"It's a long story. We're having some trouble with time here."

"Okay, then." Grandpa blinked and turned back to her. "So I hear you had a fight."

Willa stared at the ground. "Mom lied to me, and she's trying to keep me locked up at home."

Grandpa raised his eyebrows. "What did she lie about?"

"Swimming in high school."

"Ah, yes," he murmured. "You know, Willa, it's not uncommon for parents to keep things from their kids until they're old enough to understand them. I didn't tell your mother everything about *her* mother…."

"That she was a mermaid," finished Willa.

Grandpa nodded. "Yeah, I waited a little too long to tell her, and when she found out, boy was she sore at me!" He chuckled. "The truth is, I just didn't want her worrying about it too much. She's a worrier. Like you."

Willa felt her anger fade a little. "That's not the worst part. When I was little, she brainwashed me. She made me scared of the water just to keep me from swimming."

He sighed deeply. "She shouldn't have done that, that's the honest to God truth. But you have to know she didn't do it through anger or malice. She did it because she was afraid."

"What was she so afraid of?" wailed Willa. "Water? Gills? Belle?"

Grandpa thought for a moment before answering. "She's afraid you'll become like Belle and leave."

Willa blinked the tears from her eyes as he enfolded her in a big hug. "You take as long as you need here. I'll look after your mom." Then he stood, ruffled her hair with his hand, and walked away.

Willa watched him disappear into the blur of people on the street and then walked slowly to the pool. She tried to forget about Belle and Mom and focus instead on how to help Miss Trang, but as she stared into the water, her thoughts swirled together in a confused mess. She undressed to her bathing suit and stood a moment, teetering on the edge. Then she let gravity take her and crumpled into the pool.

She sank to the bottom and lay on her back. Water rippled above her, and beyond that the sky rippled too. She breathed deeply, fighting the urge to cry. When she felt calmer, she turned her head to look at the two time holes, glistening in the half-light.

Chapter Twenty-Four

In which dreams are connected and a rhyme recalled

It was sunny and bright at Gwyneth's hut. There were garlands of yellow flowers everywhere — draped over the door, hung in the windows, even looped around the goat's neck. The well, too, was covered in yellow blossoms. Gwyneth came out of the hut with a pitcher and carefully poured what looked like milk on the ground across her doorway.

"What the heck are you doing?" called Willa.

Gwyneth saw her and came over. "Willa! Thanks for bringin' this back." She patted the wooden bucket on the edge of the well.

"No problem." Willa climbed out of the well. Gwyneth gaped in surprise, pointing to her legs.

"I thought ye were a mermaid!"

"Only part, remember?" smiled Willa.

"And this …" She gingerly touched at the strap of Willa's suit. "This ain't yer skin?"

"No. It's a bathing suit. Clothing for swimming in."

Gwyneth raised an eyebrow. "That's daft! Ye don't need clothes for swimmin'!"

"Yeah, I know. It's not very mermaidy of me." Willa sighed. "To be honest, I'm not sure how much of a mermaid I really am."

Gwyneth nodded. "Bein' half somethin' and half somethin' else can be confusing. My elvish relations are nimble and quick. Brilliant archers and beautiful dancers. Me now, I'm not bad with a bow an' arrow, but I dance like a duck."

Willa laughed. "The worst part is feeling different. Like I don't know who I am."

"'Tis a blessing and a curse." Gwyneth looked her in the eye, suddenly serious. "Ye can end up having the worst parts of each, or the best parts. But every day ye make your own decisions. Y'are the person you choose to be. At least that's what my ma always told me."

Willa nodded her gratitude. Tears sprang to her eyes, and she turned away, changing the subject. "Why were you pouring milk on the ground? And what's with all the flowers?"

"'Tis Beltane tonight. The milk is a peace offering to the Little People, and the flowers are for protection. Ye can't be too careful this night." Gwyneth lowered her voice, looking around nervously. "Especially now. There's somethin' evil in the air."

"Evil?"

"It's just a feelin' I've got. I've sent Loom to fetch me cousins, the elves. I'll breathe easier when they arrive." Gwyneth sat down wearily. "I've been sleepin' poorly, I keep dreamin' of a Green Man…."

"Green Man?" Willa asked, startled. "Is his face made of leaves? And branches come out of his mouth?"

"Aye," replied Gwyneth in surprise. "How did ye know that?"

"I've been dreaming about him for weeks!"

"You too? Say …" Gwyneth was suddenly staring at her like she was a ghost.

"What is it? What's wrong?" asked Willa.

"Dreams!" she gasped. "That's where I've met ye before!"

Willa nodded. "You've been in my dreams too."

Gwyneth shook her head in amazement. "But what can it mean?"

"I don't know," Willa answered.

Gwyneth led her to the woods. "The Green Man is not just in dreams. He's also growin' outta this vine."

"I know, I saw him the last time I came here," Willa said. "And I saw a unicorn! He came right up to the well! It was amazing!"

"Sure, he comes here often enough," Gwyneth replied casually. "I'm always after chasin' him out of my garden."

"I wish I lived in a place where unicorns were so common!" sighed Willa. They walked in silence to the clearing where the Green Man sat. He didn't seem all that threatening in the daylight, with his head bowed and songbirds hopping about on his shoulders.

"There's another just like him back on my side," said Willa, and Gwyneth's violet eyes grew large. Willa filled her in on the recent growth of the vines and how they were invading the house.

"The Green Men are connected, one t'other, by this," said Gwyneth thoughtfully, lifting the vine off the ground with her foot. "What would happen if we were to cut it, do you suppose?"

Willa thought for a moment. "I think this vine is what connects your time to mine. It may be anchoring the time hole in place at both ends. It connects the Green Men too, of course, but it's also keeping the path open for me to come here."

Gwyneth let the vine fall and grinned at Willa. "Ah well, we'll just leave it be then. For the moment." Looking back at the giant figure, her face grew serious again. "The dreams are a warning, make no mistake. The Green Man does not come in peace."

"Oh!" Willa sat up suddenly as a memory flashed through her mind. "I had another dream last night! I'll tell you … but not here." She gestured to the trail, and they walked back together.

Willa waited until they were at Gwyneth's front door before she spoke again, her voice low. "A horse with red eyes always comes to warn me when the dark side is about to attack. I dreamed about him last night, I just remembered. He said …" Willa paused, remembering, then recited:

> "*In weedy bog and sunken dream*
> *Doth grow the Man of darkling green.*
>
> *Ancient evil blocks the light,*
> *Entwining all in endless night.*

> Exchange your arms 'ere dies the sun.
> At Bealtaine two minds must act as one."

Gwyneth looked at her excitedly. "Bealtaine, or Beltane — that's tonight! And 'two minds' has got to mean us!"

"Right. We have to exchange arms … give each other a weapon, I suppose. Before sunset. I'll go home and get something for you," said Willa. "We've got lots of weapons kicking around our place."

Suddenly Willa felt a disturbance rippling through her mind.

Willa! Willa!

She looked around, stilling her mind to listen.

Gwyneth looked at her curiously. "What's wrong?"

Then it came again. *Willa! Come home! We need you!*

"I have to go." She turned toward the well just as a shining figure rose from it. A woman with long, silvery hair.

Gwyneth gasped. Willa blinked.

"Mom?"

"Oh, please!" The figure rolled her eyes, and Willa realized with a start that it was Belle, but she looked so young that Willa could see her mother looking out of her eyes. It was truly weird. Belle beckoned urgently.

"I'm glad I found you. You must come back immediately."

"Is it Miss Trang?"

"Yes, but that's not all. Come on!" Belle dropped out of sight with a splash. Willa climbed over the flower garlands into the well.

"I'll see what's going on and come back as soon as I can," said Willa, lowering herself into the water. "Keep an eye on the Green Man."

Gwyneth put her hand on her sword and nodded. "At Bealtaine two minds must act as one."

Chapter Twenty-Five

Treachery revealed

As soon as her head broke the surface, Willa knew big things were afoot. Eldritch Manor was absolutely covered in vines. She could actually see them growing, writhing on the walls like snakes.

"Omigosh!"

Belle pulled herself out of the pool with a grunt. She had turned old again. "You've been gone for days."

"Days? I was away for an hour, at most!"

"Time's speeding up here. Days are rushing past like water down a drain," grumbled Belle as Willa helped her into her robe and up into her chair. "The plants have gone nuts, and Miss Trang …"

"Look!" Willa gasped. The sun was moving briskly through the sky toward the horizon, a time-lapse movie in real life.

"*That*," said Belle with a dismissive wave, "is the *least* of our problems! Come on!"

Willa hastily pulled on her clothes and wheeled Belle into the house. She was shocked to see vines covering the inside walls as well, twisting and tangling around light fixtures, bannisters, and running up the stairs. Argus and Robert emerged from Miss Trang's room, looking grim.

"Argus, where's Tabitha? We've got to slow things down!" exclaimed Willa.

Argus shook his head. "You need to see Miss Trang first."

Her room was, like the hall, enveloped in leaves and vines. Baz leaned morosely against one leafy wall, Tengu sat on the floor hugging the basilisk, and Mab and some of the fairies perched on the bedposts. Horace sat in his usual chair by the bedside.

Willa approached, her heart sinking. Miss Trang was barely recognizable. She was smaller and thinner, her face wizened and ancient, her skin transparent. She wheezed and struggled for every breath.

"Horace, what's wrong with her?" Willa whispered.

"This is no simple illness." He pulled back the blanket. Miss Trang's arms were rigid at her sides. "She can't move," he explained. "She's under a spell. A serious one."

Baz suddenly straightened and hurried out of the room.

"Someone is doing this to her?" asked Willa.

"I'm afraid so," murmured Horace.

"Is it coming from the dark side?"

Horace frowned. "Normally, spells can't be cast from one realm to another. The source of this magic has to be nearby."

Willa looked around the room at all the worried faces. *Nearby?* She turned to the window and stared out at utter darkness. *The middle of the night — but the sun just set!* The slippage of time was confusing, unbalancing. Her thoughts were interrupted by Baz shouting and pushing her way back into the room.

"I told you someone was messing with my things! I told you!"

"Baz, quit your caterwauling! This is a sickroom," scolded Robert, but Baz would not be silenced. Willa had never seen her this animated.

"I could have used it to help her, but someone snuck in and stole it!" Baz wailed.

"Stole what? Speak some sense, will you?" snapped Belle.

"Her *skin!* Miss Trang's dragon skin!" explained Baz. "Remember, Willa? She shed the skin, and I saved it, but now it's gone!"

Horace jumped to his feet. "A dragon skin? Someone may be using it to cast this spell."

"Baz complained about someone being in her room ten days ago," said Argus. "Miss Trang started showing symptoms three days later. It could be related." He turned to Baz. "I didn't see anyone go into your room, but of course I was having vision problems at the time."

"Your eyes were gummed up with tiny white strands. I still think they looked like spiderwebs, no matter what Tabitha says," mused Willa. "I think I need to talk to her again."

Willa led everyone into the parlour. Early-morning light slanted in through the front window. The vines hadn't yet invaded this room. Willa wondered if it was because the hibiscus still ruled the place, its runners stretching across the ceiling and along the mantle.

Willa called up to the knitting bowl. "Tabitha!"

"She's not there," announced Oberon from the mantle. Willa turned to face the rabbits standing guard in front of the dollhouse.

"Excuse me, please?" she tried, but they stood firmly blocking the way. Robert stepped forward, glowering at them from a great height.

"Out of the way, little bunnies," he growled and stomped his hoof.

The rabbits' noses quivered. They dropped to all fours and slunk off to the corners of the room, deaf to Oberon's barked commands.

"Man your post! Protect at all cost! Do not betray your king!"

Willa knelt in front of the dollhouse. "Tabitha! Can I speak to you, please?"

"She's not there either," muttered Oberon darkly. Willa leaned to peek in the windows of the little house, but all she could see were masses of white cobweb. The house seemed to be filled with it. She felt around the structure with her fingers.

"Is there a door somewhere? Or a hinge …?"

Argus found her a screwdriver. Willa jammed it under the eaves and wrenched upward. With a loud *snap*, a crack appeared, and Willa lifted the roof right off the house.

The interior was filled with a tightly wrapped bundle of fine white filaments, about the size of a large book. Willa lifted it out, her eyes wide.

"These strands are *exactly* like the ones that were over your eyes, Argus!" Willa exclaimed. "I think Tabitha was the one who covered your eyes, and she did it so you wouldn't see the dragon skin being stolen!"

Argus sank into a chair with a moan. "Again I have failed in my duties!" Horace patted him on the back.

"I'll bet the skin is in there," exclaimed Baz as Willa turned the bundle over. "Here, let me." She took the bundle and pulled at the strands with her teeth.

Meanwhile, up on the mantle Oberon was slipping quietly into his carriage. "Oberon!" Willa barked. "What do you know about this?"

He turned to her with the wide eyes of a guilty pre-schooler. "About what?"

In a flash Mab landed beside him and grabbed him by the collar.

"Talk, you *spineless creep!*"

"I … I don't know anything…."

"TALK!" Mab raised her fist. For a second Willa thought she was really going to slug him. Apparently Oberon thought so too, because the words began to spill out.

"Tabitha asked me for a favour. She wanted us to sneak into Baz's room and um …" Oberon eyed Baz nervously.

"And steal the dragon skin for her," prompted Willa. "Why?"

Oberon shrugged. "I don't know. Something magicky."

Willa narrowed her eyes accusingly. "You weren't very happy about Miss Trang waking up, were you?"

Oberon didn't answer, but his grimace told all. The rabbits, peeking out from under the sofa, all covered their faces with their paws.

Mab let out a gasp. "You helped her cast the enchantment on Miss Trang!" She gave him a good shaking and then dropped him in disgust. "How could you?"

"I didn't know what she was going to do, exactly," sputtered Oberon. "She just said she could make it so Miss Trang didn't wake up, and, well, Miss Trang's a dragon and ... and dragons are always the bad guys! Good guys are *supposed* to fight dragons!"

"We are *not* in the middle of a stupid fairy tale! Miss Trang is our friend!" hissed Mab, raising her fist again.

Oberon suddenly pointed. "It was *her* idea! *She* made me do it!"

Tabitha was in the doorway. She took one look at their faces and bolted. Baz sprang after her, dropping the webbed bundle, which Argus scooped up.

"Belle, keep an eye on Miss Trang!" hollered Willa over her shoulder as she ran out the door with the others.

They sprinted after Tabitha and Baz, out into the yard, past the pool, into the trees. Tabitha disappeared into the leafy underbrush. Baz dropped to all fours and snuffled along, hot on her trail. Tengu and Willa trotted along behind. Willa could hear Robert and Argus crashing along behind them, but she didn't dare take her eyes off the slight motion in the leaves ahead. She already knew where they were headed.

They burst from the trees, face-to-face with the large, leafy figure sitting against the wall. His head was upright now, but he had no face. Everyone skidded to a halt, uncertain. Even Baz froze at the sight of him. Tabitha scurried up the figure's arm, which was studded with thorns, then continued up onto the head, coming to a stop on what should be the forehead of the faceless man. She looked out at them all, and her face creased into a wide grin.

"Fools," she hissed, her black eyes glittering.

The man's face began to fold and twist. All was silent save for the creaking and crackling of the branches. Willa stared in horror as very familiar features took shape.

Familiar grey eyes stared into hers. The figure was alive and watching them, the spider still perched on his head. As if in a trance, Willa stepped forward, acting out a much-rehearsed role. She formed the thought and sent it out.

Who ... are ... you?

The silence around them was deep and empty. The eyes stared back without blinking, then the lips split apart, revealing utter blackness. Willa stared into the mouth and knew she was looking directly into the dark side. The dark grew into her eyes, and she felt its cold fingers stretch through her mind.

"No!" Willa shook her head, pushing it out. She looked defiantly into the eyes again, and summoning all the force of her mind, she pushed against him.

You are not welcome here, she shouted. A sudden gust of wind whipped up loose leaves all around her as she focused her thought and pushed again.

You must leave this place! GO!

She felt his presence falter, but just for a moment. Then a message shot back.

You are too late.

Quick as a flash, Tabitha scurried into the mouth, disappearing into the blackness. There was a moment of silence and then, as Willa knew it must, foliage erupted out of the mouth. Plant matter crashed all around them, vines and branches spilling and leaves flying everywhere, filling the forest like a flood.

She stood frozen in place, staring at the Green Man.

You are too late.

Tengu grabbed her arm. She turned and ran.

Chapter Twenty-Six

The Flame is Lit

Willa stumbled through the trees. Everyone was shouting and running. The entire forest was alive with branches and vines, leafy tentacles reaching out for them.

A vine whipped around Willa's ankle, and she fell. As soon as she hit the ground, she felt something wrap around her arms. She couldn't move.

"Help!" She twisted her head around, but she was under a layer of leaves and all was dark. She struggled as feet crashed around her. Then something grabbed her ankle and lifted her into the light. An axe blade swung through the air, and she screamed before realizing that Argus was cutting away the vines with it while Robert held her dangling by one foot.

Finally she was free, and he set her on the ground.

"To the house! Quickly now!" he barked. "We'll round up the stragglers!"

Willa ran, jumping and dodging the branches and vines until she was in the open part of the yard. Baz,

Horace, and the fairies had gathered at the back door, where Belle sat staring out in astonishment.

"Good grief! What did I miss?"

"Plants going crazy," gasped Willa. "Is everyone here? Where's Tengu?"

She heard a shout and turned to see Robert galloping toward them with Argus and Tengu running alongside.

"The basilisk's missing!" Tengu wailed. "I just found … this." He held up the blindfold.

"I wouldn't worry about him," said Horace. "I should think he can look after himself."

Tengu smiled hopefully, but Argus groaned. "Worry about *him*? What about *us*?"

"He won't turn us to stone," Tengu answered with a smile. "I am ninety-five percent certain."

"Ninety-five percent with a ten percent margin of error," added Horace. Argus grimaced.

Willa pressed on. "Where are the dwarves? I didn't see them inside earlier."

"I haven't seen them for a couple of days," admitted Argus, and the others nodded.

Tengu let out a yelp as a vine shot forward and gripped his ankle. Baz grabbed the axe from Argus and brought it down on the vine with a thud. Tengu yanked his foot free.

"Okay," said Baz, hefting the axe over her shoulder. "What do we do now, Willa?"

Willa took a deep breath to clear her thoughts. *Just have to dive in here.* "Robert and Tengu, look for the dwarves and round up all the weapons we've got."

"Right!" Robert's eyes brightened at the thought. "I know where the swords are."

Willa turned to Belle. "Belle, you stay with Miss Trang. Let me know if she gets worse." She nodded and disappeared inside.

Willa turned to the rest — Baz, Argus, Horace, Mab, Oberon, fairies, and rabbits. "We could really use a dragon right now. Let's free Miss Trang."

In the parlour, Argus and Baz worked at the bundle, trying to tear apart the strands while the hands on the clock spun around. It was making Willa jittery.

"Mab! We need to slow time down. Can you knit extra stitches in between the big ones or something, please?" she begged.

Mab flew up and inspected the scarf. Willa began to pace. "Why would Tabitha want time to move ahead like this? What's the point?"

Argus rubbed some of his eyes. "To speed up the plants?"

"But why do it *now?* She's been here for weeks," countered Willa.

Baz gnawed at the bundle with her teeth. "At least it's bringing us closer to Walpurgis Night."

"What is Walpurgis Night?" shouted Willa.

Baz stared at her. "Haven't you been listening? I've been talking about it for weeks!"

"Talking, but not *explaining!*" Willa wailed.

Baz rolled her eyes. "How is it possible that you don't know about the best night for charms and magic in the whole year?"

Horace took over. "Walpurgis Night, also known as Witch's Night, is on the last night of April. Combined with May first, the fairy Beltane, it's the strongest time for casting spells."

Willa stared. "Wait, *Beltane?* Did you say Beltane?"

"Yes, yes," Horace replied. "May first is Beltane."

"The village with the holy well! Where the vine comes from!" Willa sputtered excitedly. "At the other end of the vine, they're getting ready for Beltane! Covering everything in yellow flowers, pouring milk on the ground…"

Baz and Horace were paying attention now. "Could be a coincidence," said Horace weakly.

"Or not," breathed Baz.

"So Walpurgis Night is a good time for spells?" prompted Willa.

"Yes, spells for both good and evil," answered Horace.

"So the Green Man might grow even stronger on Walpurgis Night?"

Horace nodded. "The strength of dark forces waxes on that night. And all this activity *does* seem to be coming to a head."

Willa took a deep breath. "On the other side of the time hole, they have a Green Man too, growing from the same vine and exactly like ours."

There was silence as this information sank in. Even Mab was listening intently, her eyes wide.

"Is it possible," started Willa, "that Tabitha is speeding up time *here* so that we hit this Walpurgis thing at the same time it happens on the other side of the time hole?"

"Culminating," continued Horace, "in a burst of strength for the Green Man on both sides. That ... is not good."

"That is a whole lotta not-good," agreed Argus.

"What day is it now?" yelped Willa. "I've lost track!"

"What's the last day you remember?" asked Horace, stepping to a calendar on the wall.

"I came here on Saturday."

Horace placed his finger on the day as they gathered around. "That was April twenty-fourth."

"And I went into the pool."

"I remember the sun going down and rising four times while you were gone," said Argus.

Horace's finger slid across the page. "That takes us to the twenty-eighth."

"The sun went down after I got out of the pool and rose while we were with Miss Trang in her room. So it's the twenty-ninth."

"Not anymore!" Baz pointed out the window. "It's night again!"

"So when it gets light, it will be April thirtieth, and Walpurgis Night is tonight!" Willa looked at Horace, and they both spun around to look at Mab.

"Mab you've got to slow time down!"

She looked panicked. "I don't know if I can loop the yarn back in — it might have us going backward and forward at the same time!"

"Do it!"

At that moment, Tengu stuck his head in the door. "We found the dwarves."

The kitchen was far worse than the rest of the house. There were so many branches that nothing could be seen of the floor, ceiling, or walls. And in the nine hammocks lay the dwarves, wrapped in leafy cocoons with only their heads and feet sticking out. Their eyes were closed.

Willa gasped. "Are they—?"

"They're asleep," said Argus. "I can hear them breathing."

Robert filled the doorway, his arms full of swords and axes. "Where do you want 'em?" he asked brightly.

Since the parlour was the most free of vines, they piled the weapons there. Robert went to chop the dwarves free while everyone else armed themselves. The rabbits had their own swords, as did Oberon. Willa found her sword in the pile and held it up.

"I hope I only have to use this on plants," she muttered. She moved to the window and watched as the sun leapt into the sky.

Then it stopped.

Mab let out a cry of victory and held up the scarf, now a great long loop with a twist in the middle. "Infinity," she chirped with a triumphant smile. "I twisted it, attached the end to the beginning and tied a knot."

Horace was giving her work a close look. "The stitches aren't pulling out. She's stopped time." He looked out the window. "But we're still in this world."

Baz was looking at the scarf too, very impressed. "What kind of knot is that?"

Mab floated up in the air and spun around. "Fairy secret."

"How long will it hold?" asked Horace.

Mab shrugged. "I have no idea."

Now that the clock's hands had stopped, Willa breathed easier. "Okay, so we've got a little time at least. How are you coming with that dragon skin?"

Argus threw the bundle down in disgust, the strands still intact. "This thing is totally enchanted. Impossible to open."

Willa turned to Baz. "Didn't you say dragons burn their skins after shedding them?"

Baz slapped her forehead. "Of course! We'll set it on fire!" She grabbed the bundle and moved to toss it in the fireplace.

"Not there!" yelped Willa.

Leaves were shooting down the chimney, filling the fireplace.

"Let's take it outside. I don't want to burn the house down," said Willa. "Again."

She looked in on Belle and Miss Trang before following the others outside. Miss Trang's breathing was even more laboured than before.

Belle looked at her in panic. "She won't last much longer. You've got to do something!"

"I think we have a solution," replied Willa. "Just hang on for another minute!"

Beside the pool, they were piling up kindling, chairs, beams, and the remains of Tabitha's house. Baz placed the dragon-skin bundle on top of the wood.

"Are you sure this will work?" Willa asked.

Baz and Horace looked at each other and shrugged.

"All right, we've got no choice." Willa let out a whistle and called, "Roshni!"

The phoenix flew down from the floating attic and fanned the pyre with her great wings. Just as a wisp of smoke curled up, however, it went out again. She tried again and again, with the same result.

"The ground is too wet! Look!"

Water welled up from the ground. The woodpile was sinking into the muck. Willa felt the earth grow soft and spongy beneath her feet.

"We need to build it up off the ground." Tengu started piling things higher.

"Wait, I've got a better idea!" Willa dashed back into the house and up the stairs. On the roof of the second floor, she untied the rope to the attic, pulled it to the edge of the roof, and jumped off.

She had expected to float to the ground, pulling the attic down like a balloon, but she only got about halfway to the ground, where she bobbed helplessly.

"Um, help? Someone?"

She felt a hand grab her left foot, and Argus pulled her downward, bringing the attic with her. He tied the rope to a tree. Tengu and Baz opened up the attic door and began pitching the driest kindling inside.

"She's stopped breathing!" Belle shrieked from a window. "Do something!" Dark clouds began to swirl overhead.

"Roshni!" Baz called, tossing the bundle into the air. The phoenix caught it in her claws and flapped her wings. As the bundle ignited in her grip, there was a flash in the sky, and raindrops began to fall.

"Quickly now!" breathed Willa.

Roshni swooped up and flung the blazing bundle into the attic. They waited with bated breath, watching the attic float above their heads, rain spattering down around them.

Then the room glowed warmly, and Willa saw flames. "It's lit! Well done, Roshni!"

When they burst into Miss Trang's room, they found her sitting up in bed, her eyes alight with fury.

"She's free of the enchantment!" Belle chortled. "Just look at her!"

Miss Trang was a sight indeed. She was filling out before their eyes, and as she grew larger, her skin smoothed out. Her head came to a rest at the ceiling, and she stretched out her arms, now as big as tree limbs, and smacked the sides of the room. Vines cracked and leaves rained down.

"ENCHANT ME? ME?" The wind howled in her voice. Miss Trang was becoming less and less human; her eyes slid to the sides of her head as her face stretched into a long snout. Her great nostrils flared, and she wagged her head back and forth, scanning the room. "Who would DARE do such a thing?"

"The spider! And Oberon!" Belle cackled.

There was a flash of gold as Oberon fled the room.

"You'd best stop growing," counselled Horace. "The dwarves wouldn't like it if you broke the house they've been working so hard on."

Miss Trang snarled but stopped expanding. As the others went to help Robert free the dwarves, Willa stayed behind.

"Welcome back," she said with a grin.

"Sorry I slept in," growled Miss Trang. "So … what's new?"

Chapter Twenty-Seven

Return of the Trang

Miss Trang was so big she could barely twist herself around in the room to look out the window. "Where did all the plants come from?"

Willa told her quickly about the time holes. "A vine grew out of a time hole and spread to all this. There's a giant Green Man at the back wall, grown up from that vine, and his mouth is an opening to the dark side."

Miss Trang looked at Willa in surprise. "You're sure?"

"Positive. I felt it. And there's another Green Man at the other end of the time hole, connected to him by the vine."

Miss Trang shook her head in bewilderment. "I've never heard of anything like this. Has the dark side found a way to use time holes to travel around? And what about this spider who put the spell on me?"

"I think she came from the dark side, and now she's gone back. She was knitting and messing up time. Hold on." Willa ran and brought the scarf to show her. "Walpurgis Night is tonight, so we stopped time to prevent it!"

"You stopped time? That's cheeky." Miss Trang turned the scarf over in her hands. "I'm glad I got back before you remodelled the entire universe!"

Willa started to tell her about the dark horse and the poem, but Miss Trang shook her head. "I've got no patience for dreams and omens and cryptic rhymes. I'll leave that to you to figure out. I just want to know one more thing. What in Odin's name is *that?*"

She pointed out the window at the attic, burning and sizzling a little in the rain as it bobbed at the end of the rope.

"We burned your skin to release you. In that."

"My skin?" She perked up at the news. "That's a lucky break. We must keep that flame alive." She held up the scarf. "Once we're ready, we'll loosen the knot so night falls. The dark forces will get a surge of power, but the fire will be our refuge."

The smattering of rain increased, and Miss Trang noted it. "They'll try to put it out, of course. We need someone utterly reliable to watch over the fire."

"Argus!" hollered Willa.

He appeared in the doorway. "We've freed all the dwarves, and they're hopping mad!"

"I've got a job for you," said Willa.

Miss Trang nodded. "You must guard the fire out there. Keep it burning at all cost."

Argus blinked every eye in surprise. "There are others who would do a much better job."

Miss Trang looked at Willa, who shook her head. "No one is more reliable than you, Argus. I would trust you with my life."

Argus stood straighter, and his eyes — all of them — shone bright. "I'll take care of it," he said simply, and with a quick nod he hurried outside.

Miss Trang handed Willa the scarf. "You look after this." As Willa slipped it into her pocket, Miss Trang looked her right in the eye. "Pull out all the powers you've got, Willa. I'm not sure exactly what we're up against here, so we're just going to have to stay alert and seize whatever opportunity presents itself."

Willa nodded, and Miss Trang began twisting herself toward the door. "I want to see this plant man for myself before we bring on the night." At the doorway she paused, too big to fit through. She planted her shoulders against the doorframe. "Stand back!"

Willa shrank to the far wall as Miss Trang pushed through, splintering the doorway and sending a spray of plaster into the hall. She crawled toward the front door.

"Stop growing until you get outside!" Willa shouted, but Miss Trang didn't seem to be able to control herself. Her body continued to lengthen as she moved through the front hall, her clothing splitting and falling away, her tail shooting out behind.

There was another ear-splitting CRACK as Miss Trang burst through the front door.

It wasn't long before a crowd had gathered on the front porch. Belle, Baz, Horace, Tengu, Robert, dwarves, fairies, rabbits … everyone was there watching with wide eyes. Miss Trang lay before them in the yard, her long, lizardy form growing ever larger.

"She's back!" boomed Robert.

"Atta girl!" cheered Baz.

The rabbits hopped up and down, the fairies flashed about, the dwarves clapped and hollered. There was a buzz of optimism in the air.

"Miss Trang will handle everything."

"Of course she will!"

"Good old Trang!"

The world beyond the front gate was frozen and oblivious to the action in the yard. Willa looked up at the sun, framed by clouds, hanging motionless in the sky. Everyone was so spellbound by the dragon's transformation that Willa was the only one to see the black shape drop from the roof onto Tengu's shoulder.

"The basilisk!" she gasped. "Tengu! Don't look!"

Tengu's face split in a huge grin. Slowly he turned, and looked the basilisk straight in the eye. Willa held her breath, terrified.

A moment passed.

Then another.

Nothing happened. Tengu let out a whoop and wrapped the basilisk in a bear hug. The creature smiled and clucked contentedly.

Willa clutched Horace's arm. "He didn't turn to stone!"

"A-apparently not," Horace stammered.

The basilisk turned its head toward them and Willa found herself staring into its strange, pale yellow eyes.

She waited, and again nothing happened. Remembering to breathe, she turned to Horace. He was smiling.

"We did it!" he crowed. "An unprecedented accomplishment! This is the first basilisk in history to be trained and rendered harmless. I must write the Academy of Beasts and Apparitions about this."

Another cheer went up, and Willa turned to see a full-grown dragon in the yard. She stretched the entire width of the property and stood weakly, blinking in the light. Her legs seemed a little wobbly as she moved slowly around the side of the house.

Everyone followed. A light drizzle was falling, and the ground under their feet was sodden and muddy. Argus was rigging a large tarp to shield the attic from the rain, while Roshni watched from the roof of the house. The dragon paused beside the pool.

"Willa?" she called.

Willa pushed through the others; someone pressed her sword into her hand. She pointed out the vine emerging from the time hole and snaking off into the woods. "The Green Man is at the end of that."

Miss Trang began to cough. Her legs buckled under her, and she hit the ground with a thud.

"Are you all right?" Willa asked anxiously.

"Perfectly fine!" Miss Trang snapped back, wearily hauling herself to her feet. She gazed into the trees. "Take me to him now," she said softly. "Take me to the Green Man."

Willa led the way through the trees, flanked by Baz and Tengu, the basilisk curled around his neck like a slimy black scarf. Behind them, the dwarves and Robert hacked at the wall of vines to clear the way, and Miss

Trang brought up the rear, ripping through the foliage. Everyone else stayed behind at the pool.

"Why doesn't she fly?" Tengu whispered, looking back anxiously at Miss Trang.

"I think she's too weak," murmured Willa.

They emerged finally in front of the wall, face-to-face with the Green Man, who sat quietly, watching them. Miss Trang broke through the last curtain of vines and swayed forward. Leaning in close, she looked him carefully up and down. Then she sniffed.

"All this fuss over a *weed?*" she huffed, and slashed with her talons, ripping his face right off. The Green Man did not flinch. His features quickly reformed, and he looked out at the dragon once more, this time with eyes narrowed and mouth curled into a sneer.

Miss Trang took a step back, inhaled deeply, and gave him a fiery blast. Willa knew it was much less than she was capable of at full strength; it merely singed the Green Man's leaves. New growth sprouted and oozed over the burned bits in moments, and he smiled in triumph, lifting his arms. With a flick of his fingers, his arms shot forward, his hands slamming into Miss Trang and throwing her back into the trees, where vines slithered over her, lashing her down.

Robert, the dwarves, and Baz sprang to her side, attacking the vines until Miss Trang could struggle free. She charged at the Green Man, flapping her wings and rising just high enough to drop onto him from above. Gripping him with her razor-sharp claws, she began tearing him to shreds.

The others joined the battle, hacking at him from all sides. Baz valiantly sprang here and there, dodging his thrashing tree trunk arms to claw and bite. Willa swung her sword, Robert and Tengu wielded their axes, and the dwarves patiently hacked and chopped, but the more they destroyed, the quicker the Green Man seemed to regenerate. Wounds were only visible for a few seconds before new greenery swarmed over them. The only advantage they seemed to have over him was that he wasn't able to stand; his legs were firmly anchored where they merged together into the main vine.

Miss Trang was making no headway against him, and she was tiring. Baz fell back from the attack to focus on freeing the dragon from the branches and tendrils that kept encircling her.

Willa stepped back to catch her breath. She knew they were getting nowhere. Their only hope was the black horse's rhyme. She had to see Gwyneth.

"Keep at it!" she yelled to Tengu. "I'll be back!"

Willa sprinted back through the trees. When she reached the pool, a strange sight met her eyes. Rain was pouring down, but only in the vicinity of the attic fire, which was still alight under the shelter of the tarp. Argus held down one corner of the tarp as the wind and rain gusted around him. The others — fairies, rabbits, Belle, and Horace — were tossing pieces of wood into the attic.

"Great work, everyone! Keep it going!" Willa hollered as she raced up. "I'll be right back!" And with her sword still in hand, she plunged into the pool.

Chapter Twenty-Eight

Walpurgis Night

Willa climbed out of the well. It was twilight, and shouts and the clang of battle sounded from the woods.

In the clearing, several figures were battling the Green Man. The ground around them was writhing with vines, and two warriors were struggling to cut themselves free from them. As Willa rushed to their aid she heard a loud shriek.

She spun around to see Gwyneth leap at the Green Man, swinging her sword over her head to bring it crashing down on a branch. Her blow freed Loom, who leapt onto her shoulder. Gwyneth let out another cry, and everyone retreated, running toward Willa.

"Hullo!" Gwyneth grinned at Willa as she joined their dash to the clearing. They gathered at the well, and Gwyneth scanned the group.

"Nine. Brilliant, we're all here." Gwyneth turned back to Willa. "These are my cousins, the elves."

They smiled and nodded. The elves were slim, fair, and pale, all roughly the same height as Willa, though it was impossible to guess their ages.

"Gratwin here …" Gwyneth gestured to one sheepish-looking fellow, "thought it was a good idea to try cuttin' its head off."

"And then vines came out of its mouth," said Willa.

"Aye. Just like in the dream," said Gwyneth. "It's a blessing he can't get up an' follow us."

"I know, that's our only advantage at the moment." Willa sighed. "We're fighting him too, but he keeps growing back."

The cousins moved off to the bonfire burning nearby. "Night is upon us," observed Gwyneth.

"Yes. We need to exchange arms." Willa thrust her sword at Gwyneth. "Here."

Gwyneth grasped it and took a couple of slow swings. She nodded, impressed. "'Tis a marvellous blade."

"Made by dwarves."

"Ye can have mine." Gwyneth pulled out her sword and handed it over. It was big and bulky, and its ancient blade was pitted and nicked. Gwyneth fitted the belt and sheath around Willa's waist, as Willa awkwardly hefted the sword, nearly dropping it.

"It's too heavy for me," she exclaimed. "You're stronger than you look."

Gwyneth smiled brightly. "Hold on now!" She ran into the hut and came out again with a sturdy wooden staff. "A fightin' staff may serve you better. 'Tis rowan-wood, especially powerful during Beltane."

Willa took it in her other hand. "I'll take both, just in case." She paused, suddenly stricken with doubt. "How can we do this, Gwyneth? We have to act together, act as one. How will we know to strike at the same time?"

She was answered by meowing and saw that Loom had joined them. Gwyneth listened carefully, then nodded.

"Loom says if we remain calm and alert, we'll both know the moment." She put her hand on Willa's shoulder and smiled. "Good luck, my friend."

Willa resurfaced awkwardly, with the heavy sword dangling at her side and the long staff under her arm. Tengu was waiting for her and gave her a hand out of the water. "Miss Trang is down, and the vines are squeezing the life out of her! The Green Man is getting stronger."

Willa pulled the soggy yarn scarf from her pocket and called, "Mab! It's time to untie the knot."

Mab flew up, aghast. "Are you sure?"

"Yup." She turned to the others. "Walpurgis Night is falling on the other side, and we've got to face the Green Man at the same time they do."

"What will happen when night falls?" Belle asked.

Willa looked to Horace. "The Green Man will get a burst of strength," he said slowly. "But so will we."

Willa brandished her staff. "Keep the fire going and be ready for whatever comes. Horace, can you see that everyone here is armed?"

"You can count on me."

Willa turned to Tengu. "Let's go give Miss Trang a hand."

There was a sudden flicker of light as Oberon landed on Willa's shoulder, his sword drawn.

"May I join you in this worthy enterprise?"

"Glad to have you," she answered with a smile. Mab landed on her other shoulder, her sword and chain mail sparkling in the light. Willa nodded. "You can come, too, but the yarn has to stay here. We must keep it safe."

Mab nodded and lifted the long loop of wet yarn from around her neck. "When should I loose the knot?"

Willa looked around at each pale, determined face. There were nods all round. Willa turned back to Mab. "Go ahead."

Mab bent to the task. One end of the scarf fell free, and the stitches began to unravel. Argus took the scarf and gave Willa a reassuring nod. "I'll take care of everything here. Good luck."

The sun dropped from the sky. Willa and Tengu sprinted through the forest, with Oberon and Mab glittering just ahead of them. The staff felt good in Willa's hand, but the sword banged heavily against her legs as she ran. She wondered if she'd be able to swing it effectively.

They found Miss Trang lying on the ground, struggling against the vines that bound her. Robert, Baz, and a few dwarves hacked at the foliage in vain. Other dwarves had gone to the aid of Radsvidr and Aurvangr, who had fallen and were disappearing into the deadly green coils.

Tengu let out a war cry and ran to their aid. Oberon and Mab sprang to help Miss Trang, working to sever the vine that was pulling her mouth shut.

The Green Man himself was staring up at the sky, paying no attention to the activity around him. Willa followed his gaze.

The sun was slipping below the horizon, and the light was fading fast. *Walpurgis Night*, she thought, and drew her sword.

The Green Man stretched out his arms. As the sun's rim sank from sight, he let out a joyous howl. There was a tremendous CRACK, and his legs splintered out of the great vine, which crumbled beheath him. Freed, he rose and stood, dark and tall against the sky. He stomped both feet, and the earth shook. Then he turned on Miss Trang, his mouth opening wide like an immense black cave. Just as he lunged forward, Mab and Oberon freed Miss Trang's snout and she exhaled flames in his face.

He fell back momentarily as his features reformed, and Robert and the others turned on him, with Willa joining in. Now that he was upright, however, they could only chop at his feet and legs, and he easily kicked them away. He circled Miss Trang, trying to avoid the flames.

Willa! The Green Man has risen! The words popped into Willa's head.

Gwyneth? thought Willa in amazement.

Aye! You can hear me! Brilliant! Listen, we're drawin' the Green Man to the fire!

We'll do the same! answered Willa. She fell back, waving to the others. "The fire! Draw him to the fire!"

One by one, Baz, the dwarves, and finally Robert dropped back. The Green Man saw his opportunity, and with a sweeping gesture, he sent a wave of vines rolling over Miss Trang. Her mouth was snapped shut and bound tightly. She fell back, her eyes closed.

Another wave of foliage rippled toward them. Robert scooped Willa up onto his back and turned toward the trees.

"Miss Trang!" she gasped, looking back. She caught a last glimpse of the fairies — tiny golden glimmers above the dragon's head.

Mab! Oberon! Look after her!

They thundered into the woods. Willa hung on, looking back. Would the Green Man follow? After a moment she heard trees splinter and crash, and a dark form rose up behind them.

They burst out of the trees and galloped around the pool. Flames from the fire lit scared faces in the dark and glittered in the pool.

Willa slid off Robert's back. "He's right behind us!" The dwarves arrayed themselves around the pool, bows and arrows ready.

We're here! What now? Willa thought.

Ye must get him into the smoke!

Willa looked up at their fire. *There's not much smoke!*

Rowanwood! You need rowanwood!

Willa ran to Argus, who had his hand on the attic rope. "Pull it lower so I can reach!"

Argus hauled on the rope, and Willa looked inside. The dragon-skin bundle was still intact and ablaze in the midst of the burning room.

She heard a scream and turned to see the Green Man step out of the woods. He drew to his full height before them, a two-storey mass of branches, thorns, and leaves. The dwarves shot their arrows, which lodged in his body with little effect.

Darkling Green

Willa thrust the rowanwood staff into the fire. Immediately, clouds of smoke billowed out, white against the night sky. They drifted across the pool, collecting around the Green Man, who let out an irritated snort. The dwarves let fly another volley of arrows.

Willa drew the staff from the fire. It was ablaze now, and she moved toward the Green Man. The smoke seemed drawn to him, wrapping around his head in a thick blanket.

He's in the smoke! He can't see a thing!

Now is our chance! We must strike at his heart, but I need a moment to get closer, came Gwyneth's response.

So do I. Let me know when you're ready.

Robert, Baz, and Tengu were attacking the Green Man again, chopping at his legs with their axes. A few of the dwarves dropped their bows and joined in. Willa passed the burning staff to Tengu.

"Tengu! Keep up the smokescreen!"

Tengu nodded and sprang into action, weaving in and out of the Green Man's legs as the rowan smoke rose into his face. Willa ran around to the side of a giant leg, grabbed hold, and began to climb.

With the smoke wreathing around his face, the giant didn't seem to notice her as she scrambled higher. Thorns tore at her hands and legs as she climbed. All was confusion and noise below. Between wisps of smoke, she caught glimpses of her friends slashing away while the forest itself reached out to grasp them in a twining embrace. She looked back at Argus and the fire, still going strong. In the flickering light, she thought she saw her mother's face among the watchers, eyes wide, but that was impossible.

Willa looked up again. *Focus.* She grabbed the next branch and pulled herself up. She was high enough now and began inching her way toward the middle of his chest. Up here, the bundles of branches that made up his body were looser, and she could see between them. She paused and put her eye to a gap. Deep in the middle of the torso she caught sight of a tightly packed core — a solid wooden knot where his heart should be.

Willa positioned herself as close to it as she could get. Then she wedged one arm firmly between two branches and drew her sword with the other hand.

I'm here and I see the heart! Are you ready?

Nay! came Gwyneth's answer. *Almost … almost…*

Willa waited, hanging on and calculating exactly where to thrust. Glancing down, she saw that Baz and Robert were both down, green vines coiled around them like boa constrictors.

Ready! Gwyneth called.

On the count of three. One … Willa pulled her sword arm back. *Two …* Just then there was a break in the smoke, and the Green Man looked down at her, his grey eyes meeting hers. His arm swung across, slamming her against his chest, and the sword flew from her hand.

Wait, Gwyneth! Stop!

She looked over her shoulder and saw the sword splash into the pool. There was a different sound — a dragon's roar? — and the Green Man turned his head away from her. Willa wildly scanned the fighters below.

Darkling Green

The only eye she caught was Tengu's, who saw her problem immediately. He dropped back a step, flipped the rowan staff around so the flaming end was behind him, and flung it like a javelin. As if in a dream, it arced up through the air, and Willa's hand shot out to grab it.

THREE! she called to Gwyneth — *NOW!* — and she thrust the burning end of the staff into the Green Man's chest. His arm smashed into her again, but Willa hung on and pushed the staff with all her might, further, further into the dark knot at the centre of his chest.

An ear-splitting scream rent the air. Willa looked up at the green face tipping toward her, the mouth widening, the scream intensifying. That mouth, and the darkness beyond, were descending toward her, and she realized he meant to swallow her up. Then the world shifted, the Green Man was leaning forward, and Willa's legs swung out. She hung from the staff, her fingers slipping. Looking down, she saw the welcome waters of the pool and let go.

Chapter Twenty-Nine

"Someone has got me"

She hit the water hard and plunged to the bottom. A split-second later, the monstrous bulk of the Green Man hit the water too, his massive, screaming face looming toward her. Willa twisted and pushed off from the bottom, trying to swim out from under it, but the black mouth gaped above her, filling her vision. She made a last lunge to escape, reaching out desperately....

Darkness enveloped her, and a numbing cold seeped through her veins. Screaming voices slipped through her like a million needles. She could feel her mind start to splinter and float away. Her body seemed distant, frozen and unresponsive ... except for her hands, extended before her. They felt strangely warm, and she realized that other hands were holding hers.

Someone has got me, she thought. *I'm all right.*

She squeezed the hands, and they pulled. Willa hung on. She felt her strength draining away, but she held on. She felt the cold start to slip away.

Someone has got me, she kept thinking, over and over. She lifted her head. Through the darkness, she could see a glimmer of light that grew larger and larger until she was pulled out into it.

Warmth flooded through her, and the light was blinding. She lifted her head, blinking. She was underwater, and she was looking into the eyes of Mom and Belle. They each held one of her hands. She looked at her mom, beautiful in the underwater light, with her hair — totally silver — flowing up and around her. She looked at them both.

Thank you.

Her mom pulled her into a tight hug. Belle gave her hand a little pat. *All right. Let's get outta here.*

They swam to the surface to cheers on all sides. Helping hands hauled them out of the water.

Willa! Are ye all right?

Gwyneth! I'm okay. You too? And your cousins?

We're grand. All scratches and bruises, but grand.

Willa stared at the remains of the Green Man. His body lay the length of the pool, and at the centre of his chest the rowanwood staff still burned. His legs remained on land, smouldering, as Miss Trang breathed fire on them.

The vines that had gripped everyone had simply fallen away when the Green Man fell. Willa could see Baz crawling out of a pile of greenery, and Robert kicking off branches. The dwarves and Tengu were gathering the crumbling vines into a large pile now, right under the attic, and Roshni flew down to set them alight.

"Yahoo!" cried Tengu. "Someone get the marsh-mallows!"

Oberon and Mab flitted past Willa, their arms entwined and Mab's head on Oberon's shoulder.

"Darling, you were magnificent," she breathed.

"Yes. Yes, I was," he sighed happily. She gave him a sharp look. "So were you, cupcake," he added hurriedly. "So were you!"

"Naturally," she answered, her sweet smile returning.

Willa walked back to her mom, who was feeling behind her ears and grimacing. "Gross," she said.

Willa put a hand to her own head. "They're not so bad. And I like your hair."

Her mom raised her eyebrows in surprise and looked down at her reflection in the water. "Oh, good lord. Appalling."

They smiled at each other.

"I can't believe you're here," said Willa.

"Oh Willa, I had to come. I knew you were in danger."

"How did you know?"

She sighed. "I just … knew. Stupid mermaid powers, I suppose."

Willa laughed, and her mom smiled. "Willa, I've gone about everything the wrong way. I was just so worried about you. I'm sorry I didn't tell you everything, but I swear I was going to someday."

"I know, Mom. It's okay."

"And what I did to you, making you afraid of water. It was a terrible thing to do, and I've regretted it ever since. At the time I thought I was keeping you safe, but

I didn't really understand what I was doing, what I was capable of doing." She paused, and Willa saw she was crying. "I'm sorry, Willa. I'm just so sorry."

Willa hugged her. "I forgive you, Mom." They stood like that for a long while, their arms around each other, crying, laughing and sniffling.

"Willa! Hey, Willa!"

Willa looked up, wiping away her tears. It was Tengu, and he was pointing to the vine that grew out of the time hole. "What about this one? Can we throw it on the fire?"

"No, wait!" called Willa. "I need to do something first. Have we got any rope?"

The dwarves collected a long rope for Willa, and she pulled it into the small time hole and all the way through to the other side.

A joyful scene greeted her as she climbed out of the well. The cousins were piping and dancing around the bonfire. As she was securing the end of the rope to the well's pulley, Gwyneth dashed up to give her a big hug.

"Simply brilliant! Well done!" she gushed.

"You too! I can't believe we did it!" grinned Willa. She turned and showed Gwyneth the rope. "This runs through to my side. I think if we keep this rope as a connection instead of the vine, the time hole will remain in place."

"Lovely." Gwyneth smiled, linking her arm in Willa's. They walked together toward the still form of the Green Man lying at the edge of the wood. Two elves were pulling him apart to feed the fire. One of them called out to Gwyneth.

"Can I, Gwyn? Can I now?"

"All right, Grat, go ahead," said Gwyneth, laughing. "He's after cuttin' the head off," she explained, rolling her eyes. "Lads!"

She pointed to the hilt of Willa's sword, still sticking out of the Green Man's chest. "Your dwarvish blade was deadly! I'll fetch it for ye."

Willa stopped her. "Don't worry about it. You can keep it."

"Cheers. And ye can have mine."

Willa smiled. "It didn't do me much good. I dropped it after I climbed up and—"

"Ye climbed up the Green Man?"

"Yes, didn't you?"

"Nay, I thought it'd be easier to trip him up."

"You tripped him? How?" asked Willa in astonishment.

Gwyneth led her down to the feet. She bent to untangle the black cord looped around one giant ankle and the silver box glinting at the end of it.

Willa burst into laughter. "You used the toaster!"

"I told ye 'twas a weapon," said Gwyneth, swinging the toaster up into the air and catching it.

Chapter Thirty

A Beltane bonfire and one limited edition arachnid souvenir

The masses of dead vines provided enough fuel for a massive bonfire, engulfing the attic as well, and when Willa returned home she found everyone gathered around it, too tired to go inside to bed. Miss Trang, still in dragon form, lay curled up at the far end of the blaze, blinking sleepily. Oberon and Mab sat together on the dragon's head, holding hands and gazing into each other's eyes. Robert and the dwarves toasted each other with brandy. Tengu had found the marshmallows; he was igniting them one by one and trying to interest the others in the charred results. The only one eager to eat them seemed to be the basilisk, who followed Tengu around like a devoted puppy. Argus sat stroking Roshni's feathers and listening as Horace happily outlined the book he planned to write about the basilisk, and the scientific paper he had in mind on the topic of time hole aberrations. Baz danced in circles around the fire, rabbits cavorting at her heels and fairies pirouetting above.

"It's a Beltane ritual," Baz explained. "Circle the Beltane flame in a sunwise direction for luck and protection in the coming year." Willa immediately fell into step beside her and did one circuit before going to sit beside her mom. To her surprise, Belle wheeled up next to them.

"Time is a sneak, and a thief," she began haltingly. "And time moves quickly for mermaids. It flies by." A long pause followed. "I did come back," she said finally.

Willa's mom tilted her head, interested. Belle stared into the fire.

"I was drawn back, and … I was a foolish young thing. I thought I'd been away just a few weeks." Belle struggled with the words. It was like she was pulling them up from a deep, deep well. "I came to your window one night and looked in, expecting to see a little child, *my* little child, but instead I saw a young woman. A stranger. And I knew …" she looked down at her hands, "… I knew it was too late."

Willa's mom was watching her closely, and at last Belle looked up, her eyes dry but rimmed with red. "It was too late, and there was nothing I could do that would be any good to you. You became the person you chose to be all by yourself. I'm sorry."

"Thank you," breathed her mom, and she reached up to give Belle's hand a squeeze. "I would have liked the chance to know you."

Belle made a face. "It wouldn't have been a picnic, let me tell you. I would have driven you crazy." She looked at them archly. "Mermaids are a real pain in the neck, if you haven't figured that out already."

They shared a smile. "Except for this one," Belle added, pointing to Willa. "She's a gem. You've done a good job with her."

Mom gave Willa a squeeze. "Oh, I can't take any credit for Willa. She's chosen her own path, like I did."

"All right." Willa stood up, grinning. "I'll leave you two to talk about how wonderful I am. I want to make sure time has gone back to normal."

She stepped out through the front gate and glanced up and down the dark street. It was so quiet and still, she was afraid time had stopped again, until finally a car drove past at a reassuringly normal speed.

Turning back, her eye was caught by the glow of another bonfire down the street, in the Nortons' front yard. She could see several figures large and small circling the flames. She strained to pick out Jake's figure among them. *The Nortons celebrate Beltane?* There seemed no end to the mysteries around her, no end to her questions. Nothing was ever completely explained, and nothing was ever quite finished. She smiled. *As it should be, I suppose.*

Willa wandered thoughtfully back to the pool, where Tengu stood atop the floating body of the Green Man, merrily chopping its head off, and the basilisk watched from the pool's edge. Tengu took a final swing with his axe, and the head floated free, slowly rotating until the face emerged from the water.

The head gently bumped against the side of the pool at Willa's feet. The life was gone from it now; the eyes were empty sockets, and the mouth was shrivelling up as

Willa watched. She leaned closer to make sure the opening closed up for good.

Suddenly, spindly legs emerged from the mouth, and something black exploded into her face. Willa screamed and fell backward. Hairy legs clambered over her face and off into the grass.

"Tabitha's back!" Willa called, craning around to see where she went. After a moment there was another screech, this time from Mab.

"The yarn!" she howled. "Stop her!" Tabitha shot across the grass, with one leg curled around the ball of yarn and the scarf dragging along behind. Baz pounced and caught the scarf in her teeth, but Tabitha snipped the yarn and left the scarf behind. Tengu lunged at her, but she dodged and weaved, slipping also through Roshni's claws as the bird hopped after her. As the spider sped toward the pool, Willa made a last desperate dive, but as she hit the ground the spider sprang into the air, alighting briefly on top of Willa's head before leaping out over the water to land on the Green Man's head. She skittered over to the small sliver that remained of the mouth. There she paused and with a triumphant smirk held up the tiny ball of yarn for Willa to see.

"Finders keepers," she hissed.

There was a soft cluck at Willa's ear, and the spider's eyes widened, then washed over with grey. It was like she had frosted over, and it took a moment for Willa to realize that Tabitha had turned to stone. She heard another soft cluck. The basilisk sat beside Willa in the grass, calmly preening itself.

"Thanks," she said weakly, and the basilisk clucked back. Mab flew up and yanked the ball of yarn from the spider's petrified grasp.

"I'll bet you even lied about winning the Woodland Textile Expo eight times in a row, you monster!" she snarled, giving the stone spider a kick with her dainty foot.

The spider "statue" was put to good use. The two front legs were raised at a perfect angle for wrapping yarn around in preparation for knitting. Tabitha now sat at the centre of the mantle, holding Mab's yarn as the fairy knitted out the peaceful days to come for Eldritch Manor.

Until the next time.

In the Same Series

Eldritch Manor
Kim Thompson

Twelve-year-old Willa Fuller is convinced that the old folks in the shabby boarding house down the street are prisoners of their sinister landlady, Miss Trang. Only when Willa is hired on as housekeeper does she discover the truth, which is far more fascinating.

Eldritch Manor is a retirement home for some very strange beings indeed. All have stories to tell — and petty grievances with one another and the world at large.

Storm clouds are on the horizon, however, and when Miss Trang departs on urgent business, Willa is left to babysit the cantankerous bunch. Can she keep the oldsters in line, stitch up unravelling time, and repel an all-out attack from the forces of darkness ... all while keeping the nosy neighbours out of their business and uncovering a startling secret about her own past?

Shadow Wrack
Kim Thompson

Can Willa rally her supernatural friends to defeat an invasion from beyond?

After battling and defeating the forces of darkness, Willa is looking forward to a little well-earned peace and quiet. Unfortunately, her recent adventures have given birth to new problems, not the least of which is the task of rebuilding Eldritch Manor, a retirement home for supernatural beings, from the ground up. And no one is behaving themselves: Mab's fairies have declared war on the dwarf construction crew, Willa's Mom and Belle are feuding, Baz is running amok, Horace is living in the woods, the phoenix squawks all night long, and there's never a dragon around when you need one. To be perfectly honest, Willa is starting to think the forces of darkness were easier to handle than her family and friends — until those forces start to rise again!